D1742211

# Jango
# and the
# Evil Man-People

A story of an African Elephant
and his two-wheeler

**by**
**Michael John Wilde**

All rights reserved. No part of this publication may be reproduced, stored in a retrieval system, or transmitted, in any form or by any means without the prior written permission of the publisher, nor be otherwise circulated in any form of binding or cover other than that in which it is published and without a similar condition being imposed on the subsequent purchaser. All characters in this publication are fictitious and any resemblance to real persons, living or dead is purely coincidental.

Registered Copyright – 163566 – June 5, 2014.

Butterfly Tree Press – October 14, 2015

Butterfly Tree, LLC

ISBN: 978-0-9960615-9-9

SPACE FOR GIANTS
www.spaceforgiants.org

The illegal killing of elephants and the trade in their ivory is out of control across Africa, undermining ecosystem integrity, economic development and the rule of law. In the last three years 100,000 elephants have been brutally killed to supply ivory to illegal markets in Asia. Poaching, combined with a shrinking habitat from natural resource extraction, have pushed this majestic animal to the brink of extinction. Unless urgent action is taken, the African elephant will die out in the wild within our lifetime.

**Space for Giants** is an international conservation charity with 15 years of experience in the conservation and management of African elephants and the landscapes they depend on. We aim to secure a future for the largest mammals on earth forever, to be enjoyed by humanity forever, by ensuring that they have the space and security to live and move freely in the wild forever. We work on the ground every day to provide a secure future for elephants, the places they live and the species that share their range.

Spaceforgiants.org  info@spaceforgiants.org

Space for Giants is an international conservation charity, registered in the UK (charity no: 1139771) and USA (EIN: 47-1805681) and Kenya governed by a volunteer Board of Trustees.

This, the first of a number of short stories following the adventures of Jango, is dedicated to my children Jacqui, Rob, Anna, Molly, Coco, Imo and Gus, who have given me a lasting reason to seek magic from today and hope for the future.

The journey of Michael John Wilde is almost as colourful as Jango's story; having experienced a host of adventures and occupations travelling throughout the world. Michael's long time love of Africa includes his first hand knowledge of its beauty as well as its continuing horrors. Jango's story appeals to those eager to explore the secrets of Africa and the dangers brought about by the evil man-people.

15% of the author's profit from the sale of this book shall go to The Space for Giants Charity.

# Chapter 1

Like all youngsters Jango had always longed for the day he could ride a two-wheeler. Jango had just passed his first birthday so, like all growing African elephants, he was desperate to escape the support of his parents. Home to Jango was on the vast plains of the Masai Mara, close to the Kenyan border with Tanzania, home also to many Masai tribesmen. From there, Jango could see in the distance the rolling hills of the Esoit Oloololo Escarpment, where the sun rapidly disappeared each evening as it set in a glowing ball beneath the horizon.

Ever since he was a very young tusker Jango had ridden his brother Hugo's two-wheeler with its rusty buckled stabilisers and doubtful brakes; the damage caused by the weight of a baby African elephant. Even at birth African elephants can weigh 120 kilos, the weight of a large man – and everyday baby elephants drink nearly 11 litres of their mother's milk; enough for twenty boxes of Corn Flakes. Hugo had already out-grown the little red two-wheeler during which time he had caused the stabilisers to become badly twisted, in need of urgent repair. Riding a short way into the bush with buckled stabilisers had become far too easy for Jango. Now he longed for his father to remove them, teach him to ride, so he could explore a new world far into the Kenyan bush.

"Please papa, please, please, please, take the arms off," he tugged at his father's trunk.

"OK son, your turn to ride the two-wheeler," his father smiled with pride at his son's excitement and determination.

Jango jumped up and down like a demented grasshopper – on two wheels he could really explore distant parts of the African bush only the bigger folk visited. Stories Jango had been told excited his adventurous spirit filling him with an urgent need to explore. He would meet the dozy zebras, aimlessly galloping gazelles, and brainless wandering wildebeest, all of whom roamed the bush with a freedom Jango could only dream of.

Jango had been warned of unseen dangers of the

great wild bush, which formed part the Serengeti spreading into neighbouring Tanzania, the bush disappearing in every direction as far as his eye could see. Many of the stories Jango had overheard were about man-people who killed tuskers. Sometimes forcing them to work all day long, carrying enormous logs. Some, he had also been told were put to work carrying gigantic stones for the man-people to build themselves even bigger houses. Many of these unfortunate working tuskers having their legs chained together to stop them from escaping back to their herds.

His mother and father told him many stories of the man-people; many frightening Jango making him cuddle closer at night to his mother. Like most youngsters, Jango had developed a natural curiosity which negated the dangers of his parents' warnings. He longed to call out to new friends and to show off his talents on his two-wheeler. His brother Hugo had told him stories when he had ventured into the bush and played pranks on the brainless wildebeest and being chased by an angry mother hippo near the big lake.

"What's a lake Hugo?" Jango asked.

Hugo's response was even more confusing. He told Jango it was the biggest drinking hole he'd ever seen, which went as far as an elephant's eye could focus. Hugo also told him of the long legged pink birds who squawked and shrieked standing on the edge of the big drinking hole. Jango needed desperately to see and explore these wonders of Africa, his need to ride the two-wheeler grew stronger everyday.

"Come on Jango and I'll push you, let's see how you balance," his father offered, the twisted rusty stabilisers now removed.

Jango's excitement was obvious, he screamed with delight as he wobbled away from his father, collapsing in a giggling heap; the two-wheeler wrapped around his trunk and legs. As rapidly as he could untangle himself Jango climbed back on urging his father for yet another push.

"Shove me harder Daddy. I can do it! Just watch!"

Next time Jango made a greater distance along the red dirt track before wobbling to a halt. A great improvement, Jango was gaining confidence with each shove from his father. For the next hour Jango's father encouraged him, until he had mastered the technique of balancing the two-wheeler. That moment Jango's world changed. Balancing the old two-wheeler hand-me-down he could now choose where he wanted to play, at the same time meeting exciting new friends.

"Bed time Jango," his mother called. Exhausted, both Jango and his father ambled back to the comfort of their baobab tree which provided shelter for the family.

Jango knew sleep was going to be a rare commodity this evening; excitement at his newly acquired talent brushing away little chance of his usual slumbers. Both Jango and Hugo feigned deep sleep every morning; each day their mother poking them with her trunk until finally their eyes popped open. Today was different. Even before his mother had prepared layers of fresh Morula leaves, Jango was awake. Already he was pushing the two-wheeler, eager to ride off into the bush to explore an exciting new world. School was out today, so there could be no reason for his mother to ban him from riding into the distance.

"What about breakfast?" shouted his father, but he was gone. Jango never looked back.

"Enjoy your ride Jango...... Jango," his father continued, "remember the bush can be a very unfriendly place my son. Being an elephant doesn't scare some of the nasty man-people."

Jango laughed – "I know papa, but I won't go far. I promise!"

Both his mother and father laughed, knowing he would never stay nearby.

"Shall I come with you?" Hugo hollered after him, but Jango was now out of ear shot wobbling off down the red dirt track leading to the bush.

His oversized baby elephant bottom swallowing the

two-wheeler saddle, his hairy legs brushing against the cross bar. Ding, ding, ding, Jango rang out from the two-wheeler's rusty bell, already feeling a sense of freedom he'd never before experienced. From the umbrella thorns, rhesus monkeys squawked out as they scampered from the sight and sound of Jango propelling himself along the narrowing red dirt track.

Soon the track disappeared, Jango found himself amongst thinning clumps of spear grass spread amongst a scattering of umbrella thorns, where many bush creatures were seeking shelter from the early morning African sun. In the distance Jango could make out an approaching herd of zebra lazily searching for fertile grazing places, completely disinterested in his antics.

"Hey guys, look at me, bet you can't ride a two-wheeler like me."

Hidden amongst the spear grass, Jango had missed a two metre high red anthill constructed of earth, pine needles and clay, home to millions of hard working ants. Jango's pirouette was as spectacular as it was ridiculous. He landed squarely on his back, trunk and all four stubby legs sticking skyward. The two-wheeler lying several yards away on its side, the handlebars twisted out of line with the front wheel, its back wheel spinning madly. Resounding applause, accompanied by raucous zebra laughter broke the silence. Again rhesus monkeys scattered amongst the umbrella thorns.

Nearby, a grazing ostrich family took off, babies struggling to keep pace with their escaping mother. Jango, red with embarrassment and bush dust, rolled over feeling utterly stupid. Coyly he made his way back to the damaged two- wheeler, fumbling at his attempts to straighten its twisted handlebars.

"Like my trick did you?" he shouted to the group of zebras. "Got more like that if you wanna see."

But the zebra leader shook his head, mumbled something in zebraese disinterestedly, guiding his group away from Jango who was now attempting to make himself look less stupid.

"Always thought those striped horses were rude," he grunted to himself.

As he rode off again his pride in tatters, his determination to get away from the laughing zebras a priority. Any clear way ahead Jango could find was progressively getting rougher, for the track had long since disappeared. Now all he could do was dodge between the anthills, spear grass and foot trails left by hordes of bush dwellers.

As Jango rode south, excited by his new found freedom, he lost complete track of time and direction. Like all children his guidance system relied completely on his parents. They always knew how to navigate off the Serengeti to their wonderful spreading baobab, the family's home base for several years. On and on he cycled, occasionally bumping to a halt, head down scouring his path for unforeseen obstacles. After a while Jango stopped, looking up, realising he was now surrounded by thousands of wildebeest. The vast herd snorting and shoving, seeking the best grazing pastures. Jango was overcome with this new experience.

The mindless wildebeest surrounded him in every direction as far as he could see. Behind, the sun was beginning to edge below the escarpment. A scary realisation hit Jango, a sudden shivering fear came over him – he was lost. Where was home, where were his parents? If only he could see their baobab tree with its bare branches sticking out to greet and protect his family. He remembered what papa had told him about the baobab trees. For the black man-people believed in the magical powers of the baobab. Anyone who dared to pick a flower, for instance, would be eaten by a lion. On the other hand, if you drank water in which the baobab seeds have been soaked; you'd be safe from a crocodile attack.

Now he was alone, with the increasingly restless wildebeest still lazily grazing all around him. The Serengeti had swallowed Jango who was now just a speck in its vast wild space. Something more was concerning the little elephant. There was a growing restlessness amongst the thousands of wildebeest. The scuffing as they shoved each other to find food now turning into a rumble, as the beasts began heading south.

Rumbling, turning to a thunderous roar as Jango realised he was on the edge of a great rush of these mindless animals hurrying south. Jango had no idea he was standing amidst one the greatest migrations seen anywhere in the world: Thousands of wildebeest wildly stampeding to find greener feeding grounds for their families across the Serengeti.

The noise was deafening and the clouds of dust from the stampeding hooves were choking him. Nearby Jango spotted a pile of rocks, where he dragged the two-wheeler as fast as his stubby legs could transport him. Whatever the wildebeest were shouting was swamped by the din of the stampede. Jango edged his way amongst the rocks; all around him crazed beasts leapt high over his head pushing for the best route forward. Anthills once resembling solid towers, some taller than man-people, were knocked flat in the frantic panic to travel south.

Jango could hardly breathe and squashed himself more tightly between the rocks. The crashing around him increased with a thunderous roar like nothing he had ever experienced. Visibility was now just a few yards as the dust storm thickened, a choking red cloud leaving Jango and the rocks, under which he sheltered, engulfed in the blanket of grime.

"Mamma, papa! Help me!" were the last words he could remember as the world closed in on him.

# Chapter 2

"What we got here then? A young tusker hiding in the rocks. He looks hurt man. We should get him back to the Nursery."

Two game wardens driving behind the migrating wildebeest had seen what they thought was a baby elephant and had driven to see if he'd survived the hooves of the migrating animals.

"Better give him a shot I guess, still going to be a handful eh?"

"Stop it Hugo, I'm awake, don't poke me around. Mama, stop him, just coming for breakfast."

Jango's eyes firmly closed for he was still under the

influence of the tranquiliser dart fired into his rump by the wardens. Like anyone waking from an anaesthetic he was living in a world between deep sleep and a vague awareness - his mind a muddle.

"Come on little man, let's see those big eyes."

The wardens were prodding Jango attempting to bring him back to the real world. Jango had been drugged for the whole trip from where he had been spotted lying unconscious in the Serengeti bush near the Kenyan border. Kurt and Edward had rescued Jango when they found him cowering between the rocks, where he'd sheltered from the stampeding wildebeest.

The brainless beasts blindly fighting for pole position as they headed off the Kenyan Serengeti; driving south towards the Mara River into the more fertile grazing lands on the Tanzanian side of the river. The two wardens had cleaned cuts and the dried blood and dirt carefully washed away.

"Ok here we go, come on little man, you're with friends."

Kurt stroked his trunk as Jango began focusing on the man-people touching him. He'd never been this close to a man-person before and immediately tried to pull away. As he began to understand what was happening his fear of the man-people grew more intense. All the stories his parents had told him regarding the man-people came flooding back;

should he close his eyes and hope, or should he run? Using all his strength, still weakened by the effect of the tranquiliser dart he forced himself to stand, but immediately his stubby legs buckled and he fell forward onto his knees.

"Careful little man, let's take it easy, no rush. Let's leave him Edward. We mustn't frighten the little chap, he's just a baby."

"Just a baby, just a baby, I'll show them," he mumbled to himself as he struggled again to stand.

Kurt and Edward departed through the big heavy gate, which clanged menacingly behind them, leaving Jango apparently alone behind a wire mesh fence many metres higher than him. He was trapped. But there was food and water. Slowly his head began clearing from the effects of the tranquiliser; he could see he was imprisoned in a very large animal compound. Jango ambled his way towards the small man-made pond, remembering how his mother washed him at their favourite watering hole. He sucked up litres of water splashing himself all over. The water felt cold on his back for his senses had almost returned. Also the feeling of the sticky black mud felt comforting as it glued itself to his feet. Memories came back of playing with Hugo near their home, kicking smelly black mud over each other.

"Hello young tusker," a sophisticated voice came from behind him. "You're awake then, thought you were sleeping forever, young man."

Slowly Jango turned his head, behind him stretching his head to stand his full ferocious height, stood a handsome young male lion.

"The name's Whisper and I'm king of this place, the lion's always the king you know young tusker."

Jango eyed Whisper up and down. He was truly a handsome creature, but king, a bit too young he considered.

"So you're the king of the land eh? Bit young for that aren't you, in fact how old are you then? Bet I'm older! And my name's Jango!" he challenged.

"The king of this land is more than one summer," came the haughty reply.

"Oh, I see, just a baby. I'm two," he fibbed. "In fact I'll be three summers very soon." Jango raised his trunk and tried to bellow but it came out as a pathetic squawk.

"Well maybe you're older by a short summer, but lions are the kings, surely you know that."

"Come on Whisper we're both trapped behind this fence, so no one's a king. Who else is trapped here? I've got to get out, I need to get home."

"Well there's an angry young hippo, I think his name's Hutch. He chases the man-people whenever they come in here; real crazy kid."

"Who else?"

"Oh just the usual monkeys who swing in, try and steal our food, scream at everyone then disappear, pests I call them. Apart from them, wounded animals seem to stay until they're better, then the man-people take them away."

Like two old men they strolled away from the water hole swapping war stories of how they'd reached the compound. Jango feeling comfortable that he'd found a kindred spirit. Would Whisper want to escape? Could he trust him? Whisper led Jango around the compound like a tour guide, explaining who and what everything was in lengthy detail. Although Jango was bored with Whisper's rambling he was comforted to have a new friend.

"And here is the famous Hutch! Hey Hutch! Meet our new friend, this is Jango."

Hutch was prone in a thick layer of black mud, quietly snorting away, his beady eyes closed; as though their presence was a massive intrusion on his time and space. Eventually, he opened one eye, snorted again and rolled over, his head turned away from them.

"See what I mean, major attitude issues, let's leave him," Whisper suggested.

Behind them the sound of the massive compound gates screeched open on rusty hinges. Through the gates Kurt appeared carrying Jango's two-wheeler; Edward standing guard with his tranquiliser gun.

"There you are little tusker, must be special the way you were clinging on to it. What you going to do, ride it?" Kurt chortled.

Jango was now in possession of his two-wheeler. As they left, both wardens burst into fits of laughter as they closed the compound gates. Jango ran to his two-wheeler, lifting it to examine its condition after his confrontation with the crazy Wildebeest. It was still in one piece. He pressed the tyres, they were still hard. He would be able to ride it.

"What's that thing?" Whisper questioned, keeping his distance from the strange contraption.

"It's my two-wheeler. In fact it was my brother's, but I guess it's mine now, sort of hand-me-down. I ride it you stupid beast, just watch this."

With that Jango scooted on one pedal and threw his other leg over the saddle immediately away speeding down towards the water hole.

"See I can ride the two-wheeler, how about that?" Jango shouted turning his head to make sure Whisper was watching.

As the front wheel dug into the dark sticky mud the

two-wheeler stopped abruptly, tossing a proud young tusker in a perfect semi-circle over the handlebars, head first into the watering hole. Whisper dissolved into uncontrollable laughter, rolling on his back his legs kicking out madly. Slowly Whisper regained his composure climbing to his feet, still shaking with laughter from the mishap that had befallen his new friend.

"All part of the act, I've got more tricks like that, you wait and see," offered Jango covering his embarrassment as he pulled himself and the two-wheeler from the mud.

But his antics had not only been captured by Whisper; for Kurt and Edward had watched in disbelief as their latest charge actually rode a small bicycle. They had captured a performing fortune. Their days as poorly paid game wardens could well be over. They would offer to take the young tusker out into the bush on the pretence of releasing him, then sell him to a circus or maybe, just maybe start their own circus act. However, first they must understand exactly what the little tusker could do and gain the animal's trust. Then they would know exactly to whom they would take their new treasure. Mustafa Houssan, the crafty old devil would soon find a buyer, and it would be cash paid, no questions asked. Jango wheeled his two-wheeler back up the slope close to the gate. The man-people were still watching, transfixed by their prize. Again Jango scooted away, chucking his stubby leg over the cross bar; then once again down the slope. This time making sure he looked straight ahead disregarding his growing audience. For Hutch had also decided to drag himself away from the cool of his putrid mud for a better view of this performing elephant. Hutch moved his smelly bulk closer to Whisper who had never liked being close to him. Whisper started to edge back from Hutch.

"Know you don't like me and my habits," Hutch grunted, "but did you see that tusker?"

Whisper decided not to answer, for any reply would go straight through one ear and out the other, nothing being retained.

"Suppose he's trying to impress the man-people so they'll let him go outside. Is that his game, lion?" he rambled on.

Whisper's thoughts were already considering how Jango's talents could release him back into the big wide world: far away from the stinking compound and the company of a lazy grumpy Hippo. Whisper's mind was whirring with possibilities. For Jango's talent had created ways of escape from the man-people. However, real plans for escape were growing within Jango. He knew that it was just a matter of time before the big gates would open; then being seen as little risk he would perform on a bigger stage.

# Chapter 3

Kwange Jefferson Animal Nursery within the Katavi National Reserve in Tanzania, close to its border with Zambia, had been for a number of years a haven for orphaned or badly injured animals. It was founded by an American Philanthropist, Wilson (Paddy) Clyde Jefferson II, a third generation Jefferson, whose family controlled independent oil fields in Alaska and Southern Texas. Paddy, as he insisted on being called, due to a distant uncle who hailed from Cork in Southern Ireland; was never really interested in the family business. After divorcing his fourth wife, a Hollywood actress, Paddy decided a life in the African bush was where he wanted to spend his days.

He tried big game hunting briefly, but half way through his first safari he called a halt, realising the cruelty of killing God's creatures. Paddy decided at that moment to use his vast fortune to save orphaned and badly injured young animals. Nothing was too large or deemed too dangerous. If it could be saved, his team would give the beast a chance of life before returning it to the wild, their rightful environment.

Paddy worked with governments in Kenya, Tanzania, Zambia, Mozambique and South Africa in an attempt to eradicate poaching. He was determined to use his wealth to save many endangered animals from extinction. He would never let his work interfere with the natural food chain that was necessary for the survival of each species. That's why "Paddy's Nurseries," as most people called them were home for young animals all rescued from the African bush, many being left alone after brutal deaths within their family unit.

The Kwange Nursery was the second to be built and featured a series of inter-connecting compounds covering over two hundred and fifty acres. Three of the compounds connected to wooden shelters. There, injured animals could be cared for until they were strong enough to venture out into the dangers on the vast plains of Africa. Kwange's site had been carefully chosen, built along the Ikuu River. To create a natural environment, several water holes had been excavated, offering natural feeding conditions for those animals who trudged their way each day to the closest water.

Jango had been placed in a compound with healthy animals, treated as orphans, to be prepared for early return to the wild. Although Whisper had only met Hutch during his short stay, he'd become aware of four water buffaloes and two very small white rhinos farther along the Ikuu within their compound. They appeared to live amongst thick rasin bushes, which glowed with bright yellow flowers. Across the fence in an adjoining compound Jango had noticed a small pack of jackals, and what he thought to be a young leopard. All being carefully nurtured for a return to the wild, separated into groups to allow them to strengthen before exposing them to the reality of the food chain.

As the weeks passed Jango became more confident of his connection with the two man-people. He even allowed them to stroke him and fondle his floppy ears. Jango was feeling increasingly comfortable, for he was convinced these man-people would not harm him. As Jango's confidence grew, so did his two-wheeler skills. With the regular practice he had perfected a range of new tricks. He was no longer just riding in circles, he could now sit on the handle bars and jump from one side of the two-wheeler to the other. He was also perfecting his latest trick, riding whilst facing backwards. Whisper was however treated with more guardedness by the man-people; for they had seen even young lions cause serious injury when frightened: A tranquiliser gun was never far away.

Few could understand Paddy's Nursery policy which was one of complete love and dedication to the well-being of the animals before releasing them back into the wild only when he was certain they showed natural instincts for survival.

As the days turned into weeks the bond between the young tusker and the proud young lion grew closer. Now they shared ideas of how to escape the Nursery compounds' formidable gates. They also considered the constant observation from Kurt and Edward. Several plans were discussed; Whisper confident he would rush the man-people once the gates were open for the morning food delivery, shortly after daybreak. He would roar like the king of the jungle, making the man-people scatter. Then Jango would keep pace with him as they scampered off into the dense woodland bordering the Ikuu River.

Jango listened intently to Whisper's crazy plan. He kept insisting that the man-people would use the dart that makes you sleep, well before he got through the gates. Furthermore, a young lion would run many times faster than an elephant. One more thing, escaping in the morning meant they had the whole day to hide before dark, an easy target for the man-people.

Jango's plan was much simpler and needed his

friendship with the man-people to develop, allowing both of them make good their escape. Whisper would take his lead from Jango, making sure Hutch was well away from the gates when he sprang his escape plan. Hutch was a problem, for he had sensed the two were planning something which could only be to escape. But how could he stop them. He had tried getting closer to the man-people, but each time they backed away shooing him from the gates back to the watering hole. Hutch was clearly seen as a nuisance to the man-people being so completely unpredictable, at the same time a possible danger. All Hutch could do was keep close, watch carefully, then tag along when their plan was put into action.

Jango's daily cycling performances now drew a regular audience. Shortly after the morning feed each day, Jango was led through the gates pushing his two-wheeler. There the trick cyclist would amuse the man-people and the local Masai children who would scream with delight, rattling their ornate jewellery. Part of his plan was to become friendly to everyone, playing the dumb tusker. Whisper patiently watching for Jango to provide the signal which would trigger their escape into the great African wilderness, they both longed so desperately for.

Kurt and Edward had known Mustafa Houssan for a number of years. Kurt had worked for Mustafa at one of his safari camps, where he was in charge of security. Mustafa was not a kind man but always had a soft spot for Kurt, liking the way Kurt always showed a cheerful face to the hotel guests. On a number of occasions when taking guests into the bush on safari trips, Kurt had saved uncomfortable situations, when angry animals could have placed Mustafa's guests in danger. When Kurt told Mustafa he was leaving his camps to join the Nursery, Mustafa insisted that he stay in touch.

Kurt knew that the young bike-riding elephant would be of interest to his old boss. Mustafa had fingers in many businesses and Kurt was certain he would want to buy their bike-riding wonder. All that was needed was a way to remove the elephant from the compound and cash would follow.

Kurt waited for several days before a text message was returned from Mustafa. His message short and to the point. "In Dubai, phone 17.00 hrs this Friday."

Like many others, Mustafa ran his business in Dubai from the lobby of the Four Seasons hotel. Knowing that Kurt would call exactly on time he had ordered his two Somali colleagues to join him. If the facts that Kurt had explained to him were true then he would require the talents of his two guests to collect the prize elephant. Right on time Kurt called his old boss: transmitting a short video of Jango entertaining the Masai kids with several of his favourite tricks. Mustafa immediately understood that here was a gold mine being acted out on his cell phone. He must have that elephant.

Jango had realised their escape needed darkness. However, the gates were only opened in the morning when he was escorted out for his daily performance. Jango decided that for his plan to work, the gates must be opened just before the sun disappeared over the escarpment. He would have to stand by the gates, holding his two-wheeler, as the sun slid from view. With the gates open he could then put in place his simple plan, requiring Whisper to be on full alert.

But nothing happened. Each day Jango would shuffle up to the gates and rattle his two-wheeler against them. Try as he might, the man-people paid no attention. Each day Whisper would watch from a safe distance to avoid the attention of the man-people. Unbeknown to Jango and Whisper, each day an additional pair of eyes watched the whole affair, from the cover of the muddy water hole. As winter approached, evenings were getting dark much earlier which pleased Jango, for early sun set was their greatest accomplice.

"Come on man-people, watch me ride, come on open the gates!" Jango screamed at the top of his young elephant voice.

For once his screech had the desired effect. In the dimming light Jango could see Kurt and Edward making their way between their canvas man-houses towards the gates of the compound.

"What's all this young tusker, every night you clang that bike of yours against the gates. OK then, come on then let's see you ride before it gets too dark," Kurt smiled.

Whisper held his breath, the man-people were opening the gate, this must be their chance.

"Get ready my lion king, soon as the gates open run for your life, don't stop till you get to the trees, whatever happens, don't stop."

"What about the sleep darts, Jango?"

Jango had no chance to reply as the massive gates began to creak slowly open.

"Come on then young tusker, let's see you then, show us your tricks," offered Kurt as he swung open the compound gates letting Jango push his two-wheeler past him.

Immediately, Jango jumped aboard his two-wheeler and sped away from the gate. Edward, holding the tranquiliser gun grabbed the gates to pull them closed. As the gates began to close Whisper jumped into view already moving lightning fast from a standing start. Seeing the approaching danger Edward lifted the tranquiliser gun to his shoulder. With Whisper just ten metres away, Edward had a perfect shot at the approaching young lion, who would sleep for several hours. Out of the dusk, Hutch drove forward at full speed crashing into one of the gates. The deafening sound echoed around the compound. Edward felt the full weight of the iron framed gate smack him firmly on his left shoulder, spinning the tranquiliser gun from his hands, blood gushing from a wound above his left ear.

"Don't just stand there lion, run, leave the man-people to me," Hutch bellowed at Whisper.

Fearing for his life, Whisper said nothing as he ran through the gates past Edward, off in the direction of the departing Jango. Hutch ambled around the buckled gate and finding the tranquiliser gun, brought down his full hippo weight permanently changing its shape; no longer of use to the man-people. As though on an afternoon stroll, Hutch passed through the gates sedately, at his own pace, to begin his escape towards the trees.

Jango heard the commotion back at the compound and was now pedalling as fast as his stubby legs could take him. Kurt having given up the chase, had turned back to find another tranquiliser gun as Whisper, making his escape, appeared in view. Kurt cowered covering his head with his arms at the sight of Whisper rushing at him. Like a speeding hurdler Whisper cleared the crouching man-person like an Olympian sprinting toward the finishing line. Confused by these extraordinary events, Kurt was shaking with fear as he made his way back to the gates.

Were his eyes deceiving him, a Hippo strolling towards him? Hutch turned his head towards the hurrying man-person with complete disinterest. At his own pace, he continued his way towards the river bank and the dense blue bushes, topped by spreading mopone trees. Jango sensing heavy breathing behind him pedalled even faster into the growing darkness.

"It's me you stupid tusker, slow down we're safe now," Whisper gasped.

"Wow, you made it my lion king, I knew you would beat those man-people," heaved Jango breathing heavily, sliding his feet along the ground bringing his two-wheeler to a stuttering halt.

"Well uh…. It's not quite like that…you see….."

The sound of snorting approached them and from the shadows Hutch ambled into view, still relaxed travelling at his own unhurried speed.

"Come on idiots, we're not safe yet, follow me," Hutch ordered.

Jango and Whisper stared into the gloom as Hutch's huge rear end disappeared from view heading towards his planned destination. But Kurt and Edward had greater concerns. The elephant riding into the distance was already sold. Mustafa was waiting for delivery of the bike riding elephant.

# Chapter 4

From the moment Jango had regained his senses after the effects of the tranquiliser, all his thoughts had been to escape and find a way home to his family. He longed to splash in their watering hole with his brother Hugo, fling the slimy sticky mud at each other, then mooch around in the midday sun waiting for the mud to form deep crusts on their backs. Armed with lumps of dried mud a battle would ensue as they tossed pieces of the smelly weapons at each other. Oh, he missed his brother so much.

Now he was confused, deep amongst seemingly never ending undergrowth, semi-darkness engulfed both him and Whisper. As they moved forward, the glow from a full African moon struggled to force its light through the dense woodland. Although his friend Whisper was close by he was still a very frightened young tusker.

"Whisper, what do you think, which way?" Jango probed nervously.

"Follow me, follow the king of the jungle, I shall be your guide."

Even with his bold expression Whisper was equally scared. Whisper had spent most of his life, more than a year, tended by the Nursery. His life saved when he was found dying, having been left alone after his mother was shot by poachers. Whisper was just a few weeks old, still reliant on his mother's milk and the security she provided with the others in their pride.

Being of no interest to the poachers, Whisper was left to fend for himself. For days he wandered the bush managing to keep his distance from packs of marauding jackals and hyenas. Without food or water Whisper had collapsed near the man-people track, where he lay until a passing man-people carrier packed with tourists spotted him.

Whisper was taken to the Nursery where he was bottle fed until he was strong enough to feed himself. He could hardly remember an adult lion, growing up with man-people, numerous mad cap rhesus monkeys and Hutch the grumpy hippo as company. When Jango arrived at the Nursery, suddenly Whisper's life had taken on a new meaning. Immediately he realised here was a kindred spirit, who also needed to escape into the real world outside the compound, which had become his prison for such a long time.

Now fugitives, both escapees pushed on blindly through the almost impenetrable scrub, aided only by moonlight broken by shadows from the dense woodland. Jango took the lead using his bulk to push a way through the undergrowth, but having no real sense of direction, his course spurred on by a desperate need to escape into the open spaces. He badly needed to be away from the clinging thorns which stabbed his skin as if preventing their path to freedom.

Exhausted from fighting his way forward, Jango came against a dense clump of bushes and with all his strength began pushing and pushing. Shaking with exertion he could feel his body surrendering to the challenge, he shoved even harder. With a crash of exploding branches and stabbing thorns the undergrowth gave way sending Jango tumbling forward. As he stumbled from the bushes, moonlight swamped over them both.

"We've done it! ... argh! ... help!" Jango's bloodied feet struggled to fight the pull of gravity as the incline of the river bank dragged him down, sliding on the muddy slope completely out of control.

Above him he could now make out Whisper peering over the edge, who, caught by the slippery surface came careering down towards him.

"Whee!!!....watch me Jango! I'm a sliding lion king!" Whisper screamed with delight.

There was nothing Jango could do as Whisper sped towards him, the crunch was inevitable. Whisper tumbled laughing like a jackass into Jango. But the crash took on new proportions, as the two came to a sudden stop against the mass of Hutch.

"Look out you great idiots! That hurt. Get off me!" Hutch shouted as the three slowly disentangled themselves, water lapping around their feet.

Jango's two-wheeler, which he had struggled to bring through the undergrowth, was the last thing to join them as it skidded to a halt at the river's edge. With full advantage of a level foothold, their eyes now accustomed to the moonlight, the three escapees now understood where their route had delivered them. The fugitives had made their way through the tangled rasin and star apple bushes, finally making their way most inelegantly to the partly dried up Ikuu River. Now with the assistance of the full African moon, Jango could see they had arrived at a very narrow part of the river. Across the river bed a sand bank stood out, making up most of the river crossing.

"Quiet," Hutch ordered. "Do you hear that?"

Hutch was right. From the other side of the wooded area man-people voices could be heard, coming from the direction of the man-people carriers. As yet they were out of sight, but the man-people had sticks that shone a bright light and would soon catch up with the escaping trio.

"Now listen you two crazy fools, we have to go our separate ways," Hutch ordered forcefully. "We're different, I live in the water, it's my home. I can't survive in the bush like you."

"But Hutch, the man-people will trap you again," Jango pleaded.

"Hutch, you saved my skin. You see Jango and I only escaped when you crashed the gates," Whisper confessed.

"That true Hutch?" Jango chirped in.

"Listen to me; don't get soft on me now. I live by the river and will die in the bush. You both live in the bush and not in the river, we're different. Now get your butts out of here. PLEASE!"

Hutch turned and walked away, his sizable rear disappearing into the gloom, squelching his way along the river's muddy edge. Not another word, Hutch was gone. Lights began to flash along the river bank, man-people voices now sounded even closer.

"Whisper, let's get out of here. Come on, I'm not

going back to that prison."

"I can't my friend, you go on without me, it's water....
I can't.... you see lions don't like water."

"Don't be so stupid, it's only a little water, your paws
will get wet but not your ears, you great lump. Come
on."

Now the crackling of dried grass and fallen branches
could be heard as the man-people ran along the
river bank. Lights that had been just a glow in the
distance now began to focus closer and closer,
flashing their beams along the river's edge.

"Come on." With that Jango pushed Whisper towards
the shallow water and kept the pressure shoving
him with his trunk. "We're going together my friend,
let's get out of here," puffed Jango.

Forced by his friend Whisper gained confidence,
soon outpacing Jango across the dried river bed.
Now winter was approaching many rivers had
partly dried awaiting the rains, the summer sun
having taken effect. There was still enough water to
dampen his paws. Before he realised it Whisper had
crossed the river bed onto the shelter of the far side.

"Nothing to it my boy," Whisper shouted as he
turned to his friend.

But Jango was only half way across the partly dried
up river, his front feet stuck firmly in soft sand

where the sand bank joined the only flowing water.

"Go on Whisper, get out of here! Save yourself."

"I can see the tusker Kurt, this way," screamed Edward, his light stick now focusing closer to Jango.

"I've got him, where's the gun?"

Whisper's very first ear piercing grown-up roar was delivered as he sped towards the man-people. At last he could roar, manhood had arrived. On he sped towards Edward who froze at the sight and sound of an angry young lion hurtling towards him.

"Get out of here! There's a man eater!" Edward screamed as he dropped the tranquiliser gun, turned and ran for his life. In his panic to escape he arrived at the river's edge stumbling on hands and knees, petrified to look back. By the time Edward reached the river's edge Kurt had already made his way back to the top of the slope, running as though the devil himself was after him. Edward scrambled up the slope when reaching the top, hurtled after Kurt without looking back.

"Um, I enjoyed that," Whisper stood proudly at the bottom of the slope, pulled himself to his full magnificent height and gave one last grown-up roar.

"Did you see that Jango? My young tusker friend!

The man-people ran, I frightened them. Oh yeah, now who's the king of the jungle! Come on let's get you out of this river, they'll be back."

Like two gladiatorial victors the friends completed crossing the Ikuu River and quickly as their young legs could carry them, made their way out of sight, deep into the bush. Turning back towards the river Whisper gave one more mighty roar. Events of the last few hours had changed their lives; the two youngsters, parted from parental security, had been forced instantly to mature beyond their years. Proudly they strode on, not knowing what adventures and challenges awaited them. Not knowing the dangers following them.

Smiling at Whisper, Jango was aware that Whisper had saved him from capture by his heroics back at the river. No words were exchanged. Whisper had understood that without Jango's plan they would still be locked away back at the Nursery compound. They were even. Both brave young adventurers now prepared for what tomorrow may throw at them. But they still had company. Jango's rusty two-wheeler smothered in mud, still in one piece bouncing along between them.

As they trudged away from the river into the African night, they knew that Kurt and Edward would certainly re-group and search for them. But they had no idea that a second reason for capturing them was now being planned by Mustafa and his friends.

# Chapter 5

Escaping from the Nursery compound had been their overwhelming desire. With Hutch's surprising yet welcome help Jango and Whisper were now putting distance between themselves and Kurt and Edward. What they had failed to consider was food and water. Everyday in the Nursery they were fed by Kurt and Edward. Whisper delighted to scoff away at a selection of meat from animals caught on the wide expanses of the bush. Jango being a herbivore, each day was given branches of fresh leaves, grass and his very favourite, a bucket of assorted overripe fruits.

However, that was in the Nursery, now alone in the bush for the first time they found it necessary to fend for themselves. For Jango it was hardly an issue, the only problems he encountered were where grown elephants had already stripped the lower branches of his favourite trees. Jango was not starving, as he was foraging enough food to keep his growing body satisfied from the succulent grasses and occasional low hanging fruit.

Whisper however was growing increasingly hungry. Being still a young lion he had not developed enough ground speed to outrun gazelles, impalas or even zebra. So hunger was a real problem for a lion, spoilt whilst locked in the Nursery. On the third day of their freedom luck arrived on his side. For there in the distance circling in the heat haze were at least six vultures, preparing to pounce on the remains of an unfortunate animal.

As the fugitives approached the circling birds, the stinking remains of a young impala greeted them. Whisper raced ahead of Jango desperate to sink his teeth into the rotting corpse. As he approached the vultures, some having landed, their hideous screams echoed across the valley. Undeterred, Whisper plunged at the corpse tearing hunks of rotting meat from the fly ridden remains.

"Phew, what a stink Whisper! You're really going to eat that rubbish?" Jango shouted, already backing away from the bug invested mound of bones and rotting flesh. "See you by trees, can't stand that smell! Yuck!"

With an empty stomach his mind was devoid of any concerns of the stench rising from the reeking corpse. Whisper chomped his way through the remaining flesh, his gracious head now smothered with tsetse-flies. But the ravenous vultures were not impressed by the presence of the young pretender, several landing just a few metres away. Impatient for Whisper to leave them to the remaining feast, the vultures' screeching increased as their intentions towards the remainder of the rotting impala became clear. Whisper unconcerned roared defiantly at them, driving them back. To emphasise his courage Whisper slowly completed a lap of the disgusting heap. Then, his belly full of over-ripe meat, casually ambled towards Jango, waiting some fifty metres away, sheltering beneath an umbrella thorn.

"Wow you stink my friend, better keep down wind, that's just not nice," Jango offered, moving away from his friend.

"Well smell or not my tusker friend it stopped me becoming a vegetarian. Can you really see me sitting in a tree munching on leaves like some weirdo monkey?"

No longer hungry, Whisper was now in better mood and proud of his adventure with the vultures, striding away from the commotion, watching the squabbling scavengers fight over the remaining scraps.

For man-people, the sounds of the African night can be compelling, sheltered in the safety of a compound, guarded by experienced wardens. However, in the intense blackness of the African bush, fear of the uncertain is common even for brave young animals. Unidentified snorting accompanied by the sound of heavy footsteps on crackling foliage can cause anxiety for even the bravest traveller. So was the case for Jango and Whisper for they had never experienced the impending dangers the bush can deliver, or wondered what menace could be hiding amongst the black dense cover. For the African night offered cover and an element of surprise for unseen predators in search of unsuspecting prey.

"Do you hear that?" Whisper quivered, for the young king of the jungle was frightened.

"Let's keep moving my friend, must be the best way," Jango offered.

Quickly they moved into the bright moonlight away from densely wooded cover, a home to voices of the night. For several hours they kept on the move, ensuring to maintain distance between themselves and the potential danger from large dark patches of woodland.

Jango and Whisper had been travelling for many hours, through the baking midday sun, now feeling the dramatic night time drop in temperature, common to many areas of Africa. From round a pile of rocks shafts of light flashed across their path and as quickly disappeared back into the darkness. They had reached a man-people track. Their travels south had already taken them from well inside Tanzania, far from the safety of the Nursery, since crossing the partly dried Ikuu River. They were now by the main road running from Malambo south east towards Sumbawanga. In the distance more lights were fast approaching. Jango practically sleep walking from exhaustion, still sitting astride his two- wheeler, bewildered by the approaching lights growing brighter as they closed towards him. A car horn shouted at him from the man-people machine. Closer and closer the man-machine approached Jango as he stood hypnotized by the man-machine lights, heading down on him.

"You crazy tusker move your butt," Whisper screamed.

Whisper rushed at his friend, grabbing Jango by a large floppy ear, dragging him and the two-wheeler off the road, as the man-people machine thundered past. The vortex from the man-machine tumbling them over, together rolling down a gravel incline they crashed against a massive red ant hill.

"Close eh?" Jango gasped.

"Jango …. what the…you mad two-wheeler nut case, you nearly got us both killed," Whisper attempted to shout, his throat dry from the dust collected on their latest tumble.

Exhaustion from the day's excitement had left them in dire need of rest. After a short walk, safely away from the man-people track, sleep swamped over them both, their bodies completely drained from the experiences of the last forty-eight hours.

The Southern Tanzanian sun had already climbed high into the sky as the two friends, huddled together from their sleep, began to stir. Jango, the first to struggle to his feet, pushed against Whisper to help himself up and stretched his aching limbs. Whisper still snoring like a herd of buffalo: his legs dancing as though performing a ballet.

"Come on king of the jungle! Wakey wakey! Time to move on," Jango pushed against Whisper's back with his trunk in an attempt to rouse him.

Slowly Whisper struggled to his knees stretching his graceful body to his full imperious height. "Beautiful day my tusker friend, what's for breakfast?" he joked. "Another day on rations for me. Not to worry my overweight friend, you munch away on your monkey food; a starving king will look on."

"Oh shut up you big baby! Let's get going, food won't find us," returned Jango already moving south past a herd of giraffes, tearing away at acacia branches many feet from the ground.

As the Nursery fugitives moved slowly through the thickening bush with its immense tree cover, the racket from flocks of squawking birds increased. More and more animals appeared to be heading in their direction. Yesterday, before they crossed the man-people track, all they saw were small herds of zebra, with occasional impala frolicking past. Now they were joined by gangling giraffes, water buffalo standing and staring, together with strange horned antelopes. In the distance a small herd of elephants led by a large bull tusker, was also heading in their direction.

Jango suggested they keep their distance from any possibility of danger, and to carry on until they reached safer territory. On the horizon the attraction for the gathering of animals became visible. The fugitives had arrived at the south eastern shore of Lake Tanganyika, the world's longest freshwater lake. Fine, Jango thought, for a drinking hole, but how would they cross to get home to the Serengeti.

"Left, this way and don't ask me how but I know," ordered Whisper. "My jungle king instinct tells me that's the way my friend. Always trust a great traveller."

"Really, well tuskers know how to trek, mamma and papa showed me, and every time we were in the bush we made it back to our baobab tree. OK, let's follow your king of the jungle nose," Jango offered, moving again in a south easterly direction.

Soon the great lake disappeared from view. Vegetation once in short supply, grew thicker and from their efforts it was clear they had climbed to much higher ground. As the midday sun grew more intense the friends decided to take shelter amongst the thickening vegetation. For a while they lay quietly amongst the undergrowth; thankful of shelter offered away from the burning sun. An increasing mixture of sounds could be heard, alerting them to the closeness of possible danger. Screeching from hundreds of monkeys, chiming together with squawking from unidentified birds, all mixed into a weird concert. A strange sound joined the jungle chorus. Water, rumbling as it crashed over rocks.

Their travels had delivered them to the edge of the Kalambo Falls; one of the largest single drop water falls in Africa. Permanently in flood, the water cascading over 230 metres into the Kalambo River. At its widest, the river opened into a gorge over one kilometre wide and five kilometres long. The Kalambo River finally arriving on the Lake Tanganyika Rift Valley. Calmed by the mixture of the sounds from the falls, certain no danger threatened them; the two friends slipped into a deep midday sleep, comforted by their sheltered surroundings and the shade provided by thickening cover.

For all the good work and money Paddy Jefferson

had injected into the fight against poachers, working with a number of Central and Southern African nations, it was clear the poachers were winning the battle for control of the ivory trade. The figures were scary. In 2011, over twenty years since ivory trading had been banned, 23 tonnes of ivory was captured and then destroyed in Africa. Although the captured ivory didn't find its way to its market, primarily in China and Thailand, over 2,500 male elephants in their prime had been slaughtered. Some shot and some as in Zimbabwe indiscreetly poisoned. But the elephant ivory trade was not the only illegal trade prospering. Rhino horns were another prize much sought after as an unproven cancer cure in Vietnam and as ornamental dagger handles in the Middle East.

Poachers were mostly illegal Africans moving between countries in search of easy money. Being shot by wardens or the border police seemed of little importance, a risk worth taking. Nothing seemed to concern the increasing number of evil poachers: ivory, rhino horn, rare birds, snakes; in fact anything where an unscrupulous trader would pay cash was their life blood.

Jango's parents had recounted hand-me-down stories of fully grown elephants taken from their herds and killed only for their tusks. To a young tusker these stories meant little, as Jango had been brought up in a very close family, sheltered from the horrors that can form part of the food chain.

However, the horrors inflicted by the cruel man-people provided the greatest danger. Yet here was the issue confusing Jango.

At the Nursery, Jango had been treated kindly by the two man-people, who had saved him after being injured on the Serengeti by the rampaging wildebeest. Both had pampered Jango giving him the opportunity to improve his skills on the two-wheeler. Everyday they fed him, fussed over him, treated him as their special pet. They had repaired his two-wheeler, even re-painted it. Today Jango's two-wheeler was still working, the bright red paint now faded but still in good working order, despite the escapades during his travels.

If only Jango could understand. Kurt and Edward in their own greedy way were equally dangerous man-people. They had shown kindness to the animals under their control and at the same time they had made an illegal deal with the unscrupulous trader Mustafa Houssan. What was unknown to Kurt, Edward or indeed Jango, was that the two Somalians who had seen Kurt's video in Dubai, were part of a pirate gang who would capture anything to ransom and raise cash for their criminal bosses.

Geography and country borders were not a specialty to either elephants or lions; so Jango and Whisper were unaware that since leaving Paddy's Nursery their journey had brought them to the border between Tanzania and Zambia. Invisible borders had little use in their navigation system, for they wished only to return to Jango's home.

"Do you hear that? What's that bellowing?" Whisper queried, standing up.

Jango cocked an ear in the general direction of the bellowing. "Whisper that's an elephant shouting for help, come!"

With that Jango still armed with his two-wheeler pushed his way along the track running away from the endless roar of the Kalambo Falls, Whisper in hot pursuit. The bellowing had turned to screaming, a sound Jango remembered when his uncle had been hit by a man- machine on the man-track near their home. On they ran until an opening in the trees led them into a clearer expanse of open bush. There, just a few yards away stood a massive bull elephant with beautiful curved tusks. Ten man-people were stabbing long sticks into his under belly as he screamed with pain. Nearby, a large man-people truck was cruising around, loaded with more man-people standing in the back, two holding tranquiliser guns.

"Come on Jango," shouted Whisper, "you take the man truck and I'll chase the others away."

With that, roaring as he'd never done before Whisper the Great - as the story would develop in years to come – charged at full speed at the man-people, some still prodding into the wounded elephant.

"OK watch me great lion king," hollered Jango squeezing out his best bellow, trunk pointing forward at his target, pedalling as fast he could towards the man truck.

Their spontaneous plan had the desired effect, the ten man-people attacking the large old bull, immediately ran for their lives. Three attempted to leap on to the man truck, without success, tumbling to the ground, left alone and frightened. The driver of the man truck had already decided to make his escape. The sight of a charging elephant riding a bike was just too much: even if the charging beast was a young tusker. Petrified, the driver swerved away from Jango, his violent change of direction tossed the gunmen standing in the man truck around like peas; the guns from their hands crashed into the bush.

Within minutes there was no sight of the man truck, just a cloud of dust and three man-people, having dropped their spears, running for their lives. The other attackers now hiding in the relative safety of the undergrowth. One of the slower man-people sporting deep bleeding marks on both legs, as result of Whisper's badly timed leap. Missing the man-person's back but delivering a souvenir to both his legs.

"Yes! Yes, the lion king strikes," Whisper let out

another roar, "What a team! Eh? Jango?"

But Jango was frozen to the spot, quivering from the realization of the stupidity of their actions. How close he had been to a serious collision with the man truck. Worse still, he had attacked man-people each armed with tranquiliser guns that make you sleep. In their excitement both had forgotten the enormous old bull elephant, they had just rescued. The old bull staggered around aimlessly, reeling from the effect of the poison spears the man-people had driven into his bleeding under belly.

# Chapter 6

For several years poachers had been aware wardens had been ordered to shoot them on sight. For the poachers this was a serious problem requiring a different approach. Their issue how to trap then kill a suitable bull elephant target, remove the precious ivory, and then make it from the scene of the crime without marking their position. Firing their powerful rifles could be heard over some distance across the relative silence of the bush. Wardens could arrive from any direction. But now the wardens had the use of helicopters laden with modern search technology. The evil poachers' chances of escape with their haul of ivory becoming increasingly risky. So aware of the risks they were taking, poachers sought new ways to kill the giant tuskers.

The answer was simple yet brutal, returning to ancient ways used by their forefathers - poison. Callously they would add large quantities of poisons to selected drinking holes. Then the poachers had a simpler task, watching as their prey keeled over suffering a painful death. There was also an awful side effect of these hideous crimes. Not only did their target carrying the precious ivory die, but other innocent beasts died as well. The second method adopted by the poachers in an attempt to keep their location secret was to use spears or arrows dipped in the deadly poisons. This was far riskier for the poachers for it required one to one contact with a furious and unpredictable elephant. For tribesmen were fully aware that elephants were probably the most dangerous wild animals, with no natural predators other than man-people.

Sometimes the great tuskers scored battle victories, leaving some of the poachers wounded and on occasions dead. Inevitably poachers won the war. Their methods causing many brave tuskers to die slow and extremely painful deaths.

Whatever the challenges set by the poachers, people such as Paddy Jefferson were determined to stop the evil trade. For many rare animals were heading for extinction. Already the rhino stocks had dwindled to danger levels. Fewer roamed free, most now existing within nature reserves in an attempt to protect them from poachers, who were continually prepared to risk life and limb to trade ivory and Rhino horns.

"Jango! Quickly he's getting away, after him!" Whisper shouted as he started after the giant tusker, who was now unsteadily making his way towards the watering hole back along the track.

"OK, but careful he looks hurt; I saw my uncle hurt once by the man-people and he was so mad he tried to whack us with his trunk before he toppled over," Jango remembered.

"Don't forget I'm the king of the jungle young tusker," he shouted as he passed the giant tusker and turned to face him. "Wow, stop old man we're here to help! Didn't you see me chase the man-people away?" Whisper shouted, standing his full height just a few metres in front of the towering tusker, bravely blocking his path.

"Move away young fella! Can't you see I'm dying, got a long way to go," the giant tusker returned struggling for breath under the influence of the poisonous wounds.

Mustering all his strength the giant tusker started to move forward, but his knees buckled, falling on to his side swishing a massive cloud of dust and flies skyward. Gasping from his run to catch up, Jango arrived to join Whisper.

"OK old man we're here to help. Whisper I know what to do, just watch but I'll need your help," Jango ordered.

Fortunately, the giant tusker stumbled just a few yards from the edge of a watering hole. Jango now in charge ran the few yards to the waterhole and using all his strength sucked up the muddy water, rushing back to the fallen tusker. With a great puff Jango splashed the muddy water against the bloodied wounds, at the same time rubbing the tip of his trunk to remove the blood. Watching in disbelief Whisper stood mesmerized as his friend repeated the washing process, for each of the wounds.

"OK your turn now my royal friend," he ordered Whisper. "All you do is lick the wounds clean with your ugly tongue. Hurry, you can also be a great healer as well as a great warrior."

Reluctantly, Whisper moved closer to the giant tusker, who, even lying on his side towered over the nervous young lion. After a few false starts and a nudge from Jango, Whisper began licking the open wounds. For several minutes he stuck to his task occasionally standing back to admire his work.

"Ok, now for the final treatment, which I must do," Jango continued peering at Whisper's handiwork.

Back to the watering hole he went, but this time returning with slimy black mud which he carefully pressed into each of the wounds. The full treatment took several trips until Jango was satisfied.

"That's it, like my uncle we'll have to wait and see if he lives. Nothing more we can do but wait," Jango informed Whisper.

The great tusker's eyes were blinking as he drifted in and out of consciousness, his breathing slow as his massive body fought the effects of the poison.

Day time turned into the black African night as the two friends lay beside the sick body of the giant tusker. Both determined to stay with him, intent on nursing the magnificent beast back to health. Somehow the night time sounds had taken on a new meaning. For even a massive bull tusker could fall prey to hungry predators, if unable to defend himself. There was an uncertain safety from the blackness now surrounding them. But once day arrived it would be a short time before flocks of blood thirsty vultures would begin to circle over the dying beast. As much as they tried to stay guard over their new friend, the day's gruelling events had taken its toll, both friends collapsed into a deep sleep.

"Can't sleep all day, you know, my young warriors, time to move on," standing over them like a mountain the giant tusker had regained enough strength to stand on all fours. "Come on my young friends. Wakey! Wakey!" he tried again.

This time both Jango and Whisper jumped to their

feet, shocked to find their patient apparently on the mend. Nervously they backed away, uncertain what to do or say.

"Now my friends I think I need to thank you for saving my life. I could be heading for the elephants' graveyard if it weren't for you, young fellas," he stuck out his trunk towards them.

"Thank you, whatever you want, I'm your friend forever," his voice trembled. "Now," his voice steadied as though no one should see the emotion welling up, "introductions I think, my name's Tulu and I was the leader of my herd, but who knows where they are now. And you are?"

Jango reached up to his full height. "I'm Jango, sir. And this is my best friend Whisper. We're on our way up North to the Serengeti where mamma and papa live."

"North you say, are you sure and please, not sir! Call me Tulu, once the king of the herd now a sick old man," Tulu offered.

"Yes back home Tulu," Whisper chipped in, "not my home but Jango and I are brothers. So where he goes, I go."

"Follow me my young travellers I shall be your guide and get you home. Come!" Tulu continued. Without further hesitation Tulu turned back down the track towards the open space in the bush where he'd been attacked.

With the scorching Zambian sun reaching its zenith it was obvious to both Jango and Whisper their new friend and guardian was struggling. His enormous feet dragging dust clouds as he attempted to maintain the pace he was determined to set.

"Think we should ask him to stop and rest?" Whisper suggested out of Tulu's earshot.

"He won't do that, he's too proud, leave it to me," Jango insisted.

Leisurely Jango sidled up to their massive friend, who appeared lost, marching aimlessly staring firmly ahead.

"Excuse me sir," Jango asked, "can we stop for short time? You see Whisper needs meat, he's getting weak. Not for long....please."

Tulu turned his head towards Jango. "OK, but not long, we've got to catch up with my herd."

No mention of how he was feeling, but secretly relieved they could rest a while. Jango turned to Whisper who caught his smile, for he knew their plan had worked. Tulu was indeed a very brave old tusker, but still suffering the consequences of his brutal attack.

As the hot Zambian sun dropped from the sky Jango awoke from another deep sleep, hungry but ready to move on. Whisper always content to have extra sleeping time, stirred slightly but remained lying on his side. However, the group couldn't move yet, as Tulu was still sleeping; his large frame covered by colourful birds, busily pecking away the bugs swarming across his leathery hide. Although he had shown a brave face, it was obvious the aging tusker was still in pain.

Jango had seen his uncle take several days to recover, not from poison but deep cuts to his legs after the mishap with a large man truck. Jango's uncle a victim of a drunken man truck driver who fell asleep, leaving the road and piling into his uncle's herd. Its load of cement bags had burst open, creating a choking dust cloud. Uncle was the only victim, but the herd broke up as the other adults and baby elephants scattered from the accident, fearful that more problems could ensue.

"Well, well! What do we have here?" A large male chimpanzee silently swung down from the nearby acacia tree. "Sorry to frighten you, I've been watching you for some time. I'm Benjamin, Benny to my friends," the chimpanzee offered.

"Our friend's not well, the man-people attacked him," Jango replied.

"And what do you want monkey?" Whisper stirring from his sleep queried gruffly.

"Wow young fella, well I watched the way you

helped the big fella. You're good boys," Benny came back. "Just wanna be friends, I guess you could need some help."

Jango turned to Whisper amused by his suggestion, it being common knowledge that lions and monkeys are most unlikely to become friends. Whisper shrugged holding his head back in his most imperious way.

"OK, but don't expect me to like him, they remind me of the man-people," Whisper walked away, looking at Tulu's wounds and snarling at the birds pecking away on the giant tusker's back.

"Be back soon," Benny shouted, swinging away through the branches and quickly disappearing into the undergrowth.

"What do you make of that Whisper?" Jango questioned.

"Never trust a monkey, not my sort of friend," Whisper huffed, "still be OK for you fruit eaters, you can all go sit in the trees together, hanging around like fruit bats." Less than impressed by the intruder into their lives, Whisper rolled back on his side, closed his eyes, snoring again.

Jango reflected he had pushed, sometimes ridden, his two-wheeler all the way from the banks of the Ikuu River. They had escaped pursuing wardens, due to Whisper's courage in frightening the man-people. Now, standing next to Tulu, Jango thought about the days he had spent travelling. Those first exciting steps of freedom when his parents had allowed him to ride away from home into the bush. The fear he felt getting lost on the vast Serengeti. His good fortune, finding the pile of rocks that saved him from thousands of stampeding wildebeest. But there were happier days too. Performing tricks for the two man-people and the colourfully adorned young Masai outside the Nursery compound. Now with his best friend Whisper, they were miles from home, guided by an old tusker who carried battle scars from his confrontation with the evil man-people.

Whisper was still snoring, a habit Jango found irritating yet somehow comforting, knowing his friend was close by. But his urge to ride his two-wheeler was overwhelming. Nearby a track lay straight and wide with only a few pot holes where the rains had collected. So what was preventing a short trip? They wouldn't miss him for a while. His heart began racing with excitement. Desperate to explore rising ground, he cycled off along a well-trodden path. From the foot prints it was clear many animals had travelled to and from the waterhole where they'd treated Tulu.

How free he felt pedaling away into the bush, the wind pushing back his floppy ears, his legs pumping the pedals as he sped farther, along the red dirt track. Across the plain he could see smoke rising from distant man buildings. Closer by, what appeared to be small buffalo creatures grazing on the verdant grass. Jango soon arrived at a high point. Looking back he could spot the clump of trees where he'd left Tulu and Whisper sleeping. The view was amazing. Past the spot where his friends slept he could see a large shining patch which disappeared into the distance. Jango was looking back northwest at the bottom corner of Lake Tanganyika, which they had passed several eventful days ago.

"And what's a tasty young tusker doing here?" A growling voice came from a group of six scabby hyenas who had taken position in an aggressive arc formation, blocking his path.

Two of them broke rank, sidling towards him to create an extended "U" attack formation completely blocking his escape.

"Think he'll taste good?" snarled another.

"Oh yes I've not eaten for two days, very tasty I'm sure," came further snarling agreement from one of the hyenas who had now moved behind Jango, to complete the cordon around him.

Jango was now surrounded by an increasing pack, numbering around twenty snarling brutes. So what to do? He could jump on his two-wheeler attempting to outpace them back down the track. But for sure they would tear their razor sharp teeth into his hide as he fought past them. His father had warned him never to play with hyenas. For hyenas could not be trusted, simply killing machines, hunting in packs, never alone.

"What's this thing tusker, your new weapon?" the leader laughed to himself, pointing at Jango's two-wheeler.

"We are really frightened! We are!" The voice, full of sarcasm from behind him. "Come on, let's get on with it, feeding time!"

As with all hyenas forming to attack there was uncertainty. Who would make the initial lunge, to secure the first lump of flesh? As though walking in a mine field, the pack began edging even closer. The leader now no more than five metres from Jango, baring his razor teeth ready for the first attack. Jango was petrified and shaking with fear, conscious of his foolish mistake; stupidly leaving the safe company of Tulu and Whisper, to ride his two-wheeler. He knew that fearless starving hyenas would tear him apart, and his young life would end on a dusty track miles from home. His father said there was no reason to be brave in such a situation; run and hope for the best. Jango was not as brave as he thought. Eyes closed, his life played out before him. His family would be waiting, the chattering monkeys that annoyed his father, would still be sitting in the baobab.

As though carefully choreographed, three deafening sounds halted the hyena's attack. Whisper at full speed, teeth bared, his roar sufficient to frighten the bravest foe. Thundering along just a short distance behind, bellowing at full volume resonating across the bush hurried Tulu. A new ally had also arrived from the surrounding trees. Swishing across the face of the hyenas supported by overhanging branches, Benny screeched at full voice, a sickening noise sufficient to scare away even the bravest monster. Whisper's cavalry had arrived. Jango's best friend was pelting down the track in full attack mode. A short way behind the massive form of Tulu, his trunk raised in anger a fearsome sight for anyone in his path. Jango was still frozen in fear and could not believe his life was being saved. There was now a chance he would see his family again.

"It's OK young Jango," squawked Benny from the safety of an acacia, "they're cowards. Here come your friends."

By the time Tulu arrived the hyenas had scattered in all directions apart from one sickly male, which Tulu tossed in the air with his shining tusks. Whisper caught the sickly snarling beast, summarily ending his days of attacking defenceless animals. For Whisper had solved his supper issues for another day.

"Well that was fun young tusker my lad, haven't had that much fun in years. Looks as though our young lion friend won't be complaining he's hungry for a while. And who are you little monkey? Saw what you did, very brave!"

"Excuse me you great lump, I'm a chimpanzee not a monkey," Benny snapped.

"Oh dear! Offended you, have I? Fine! Chimpanzee it is. I'm Tulu so let's try again, shall we?" Tulu chuckled.

By the time a sated Whisper re-joined the enlarged group, the sun had dropped over the horizon, Africa's lights extinguished for yet another eventful day. Benny, a new friend had joined Jango, Whisper and Tulu. Together they had driven off the evil man-people attacking a brave old tusker; then saved Tulu's life with their mud medication treatment. Jango and his two wheeler had ridden into danger, only to be rescued by his army of friends.

As darkness completely enveloped them, sleep was a far distant consideration. An adrenaline rush fighting off the hyenas left them all unable to sleep. No longer did Jango and Whisper fear the sounds of the Zambian night. Resting with Tulu had given them a safety blanket, comforting them for the first time since their escape from the Nursery. Like all strangers meeting for the first time, family history and life experiences formed part of the evening's chatter.

As they talked late into the night, the group, now including Benny, became more comfortable with each other. Whisper always a chatterbox, rattled on explaining his story after his mother was killed. His time in the Nursery before his best friend Jango had arrived, including his lyrical version of their exploits. Much to Jango's embarrassment Whisper's account of their escape was somewhat too colourful. Nevertheless, among close friends his description was close enough for Jango to smile, letting Whisper have his moment.

When Jango's turn came around, he found it difficult to discuss his family. For much as he was enjoying the experiences of his travels, deep down he was hurting. Jango had explained to Tulu they would continue travelling north until they arrived back on the Serengeti, close to the Esoit Oloololo Escarpment where he would be reunited with his family. Whisper would then have a family he'd never had. His brother Hugo had never considered a lion playmate, but Jango was convinced once they met, a lifelong friendship would follow.

Now unaware of the dangers and sounds of the night the four continued swapping stories. Tulu, who at first had listened, now began to share some of his life experiences with his two young friends and their new chimpanzee friend Benny. For in Tulu's opinion, monkeys they were, whatever smart name they might choose. Tulu continued with his story, explaining he had led his herd for several years and fathered a number of children, all who had stayed with their mothers before making their way into the world.

More stories of the horrors that man-people inflicted on tuskers were told. Tulu had seen many of his friends killed, as the man-people cut off their tusks. Once, he had chased away a group of man-people as they attacked a large old tusker, crippled by noises from the man-people sticks that kill. Tulu choked back his emotion, as he remembered how his friend had finally died, being forced to watch him helplessly. For several minutes they all lay silent, thinking of the dangers that lay waiting from man-people who cared nothing for the lives of innocent animals.

"North?" Tulu brought them back to the moment. "Jango did you say you're heading north back home to your parents?"

"Why don't you travel with us?" Jango suggested.

"But you're heading south you stupid young tusker," Tulu laughed. "You're going exactly the wrong way. How long have you been travelling south?" Tulu was now shaking with laughter. "OK, sorry my friends but I should have realised. No matter, we'll get you back home. I've an idea which will make it quicker for you. Now get some sleep and we can start at first light – North, oh my word!"

Jango was already munching his way through savannah grass when Tulu began stirring from his slumbers. Benny was settled in a morula tree tearing away at its leaves and fruits. Whisper sated from his jackal meal last evening, was rolling around in his sleep entertaining Jango with his snorting and leg waving.

"Come on great lion king! Wakey! Wakey! Time to go North my friend," Jango ordered shoving him with his trunk.

Whisper eventually opened his eyes stretching his graceful body to its great length. As he stood to his full height he became aware that Tulu and Jango were already wide awake, staring at him as he went through his morning stretches. Most jungle cats keep their bodies in good order by a series of exaggerated stretches, ensuring their bodies are ready and conditioned for chasing their prey. Whisper was no exception treating his friends to an exhibition of his exercises.

"Now my friends we're travelling south for a few days, then you will have a surprise provided by the man-people, which will take you back home," Tulu offered.

Jango and Whisper looked at the back end of the massive old bull tusker as he ambled away across the Zambian plains, heading south. His leathery tail swishing at an endless supply of tsetse-flies. Benny, having run out of trees to swing from, was now perched like a race jockey on Jango's back, much to the irritation of Whisper.

For several days they travelled south, little said

between the four travellers. For food and water were their priorities. Jango and Tulu searching across the sparse plains for sufficient greenery to supply the bulk required each day. Benny disappearing into the branches of passing trees some way above the reach of the two elephants. When he could, he tossed from the higher branches ripe fruit for them to pick up.

However, Whisper was becoming weaker for his last meal had now been three days ago. Each day he searched the horizon for circling vultures or buzzards hoping to find another carcass. On the fourth day as the sun started to slip from view they approached a sheltered watering hole.

A number of water buffalo had finished feeding, trudging away with their young calves in tow. Toward the back of the herd, two youngsters were struggling in the thick mud, their legs dragged down by the clinging mire. The smaller of the two calves had made it from the mud and was beginning to gain momentum, when Whisper smashed into the youngster. Now under attack from Whisper, the youngster began squealing, the sound carrying to the disappearing herd. One of adult water buffalos hearing the fearful scream turned back for the stricken baby. Whisper was ready and turned towards the angry beast charging towards him to save her calf. However, help for Whisper was at hand. Tulu determined his friend would eat, moved into the path of the charging buffalo, veering it off course, protecting Whisper from the full force of the angry mother. The second baby now free from the mud passed well clear of Whisper. Realizing there was no hope for her calf with Tulu separating them, she edged her other baby slowly and reluctantly back towards the waiting herd. Africa's food chain had once again provided Whisper with rations enabling him to survive the journey.

"It's very simple my young friends. Man-people have train trucks that run on very long hard stick things. It's pulled by a man train that puffs thick black smoke. But never fear it can take you north to your family," Tulu advised. "Behind the man train will be trucks that you can hide in, then jump out when you get home. Now this is what we are going to do," Tulu continued.

The two friends' eyes wide open, aghast as he went through his plan which to be executed in the dead of night. Tulu had forgotten about the sickness from the man poison, and considered himself fully fit and ready to out march any youngster. In truth the pace he had now set for their trek south to the railroad was telling on his old bones.

When they first caught sight of a glow in the sky, it was like nothing they had ever experienced. The group were closing in on Lusaka, the main city in Zambia. From the lower plains they had climbed over 1,200 metres above sea level to reach the outskirts of the city. They would have to take great care as they approached their destination, for Lusaka was home to nearly two million man-people, everyone a potential danger. So caution was the byword, and travelling under the cover of darkness was vital if they were to follow Tulu's cunning plan.

Smells from some of the man buildings they passed at night were driving Whisper crazy. Hungry again, Whisper was in need of food. This time there was no need to follow his natural instincts, for Benny was a seasoned pilferer. He was in his element and showed Whisper how to scavenge food from bags and bins the man-people threw out at night. Some of the leftovers made Whisper feel sick, but with Benny's help they managed to unearth sufficient to keep the growing beast from starving.

Tulu's great plan called for patience. Waiting for the moon to be covered by thick cloud would offer them a better chance. For several days the four waited patiently in the bush, hidden from view in a large clump of reeds close to a small river. Occasionally under cover of darkness Benny made raids on the man-people rubbish, usually returning with morsels for Whisper. A respect was developing between the lion and the chimpanzee. The new friendship amused Jango.

On the fourth night dark rain clouds covered the moon leaving the land in perfect darkness. Tulu, ever cautious, warned that as they approached their target, man lights would brighten up the sky;

absolute silence must be observed.

"My plan's fool proof," Tulu whispered, "we wait until there's no moon, and then we just walk into the man train place, climb into a truck and the man-people will take us north. Stay close to me and don't make a sound," Tulu ordered.

Although he would never acknowledge the fact, his plan was completely crazy. For if they were spotted there was a good chance they would be captured and the man-people would certainly treat them badly. At worse they would kill Tulu for his tusks, for him this could be his last adventure if it went badly wrong.

Through the darkness, man lights high from the ground were lighting up the train place. In the distance the biggest man machine they had ever seen came into view, joined together like a long snake. As they approached the man train, the size took their breath away. They had seen many man trucks, but nothing like this. These towered over them snaking away into the distance. Jango, Whisper and Benny stood motionless, frightened of what was happening.

"Come on follow me," Tulu whispered.

Making their way along the endless man trucks, Tulu enjoyed the whole escapade, guiding them towards a slope rising up the side of one of the man trucks. As they topped the slope, Tulu edged towards an open door showing them access directly inside the truck. From their higher vantage point, they could now see that some of the trucks were covered like houses and some open to the skies. Many of the open trucks loaded with strange shapes.

"Quickly this one," Tulu ordered, as the three friends nervously poked inside the truck. In the pitch blackness there was no indication what else they would be sharing the space with. But if this was the way back to the north, then Jango must take the risks.

"You OK in there?" Tulu questioned, not waiting for an answer the door closed with a slam.

"Tulu what's going on, aren't you coming?" Jango's muffled voice shouted out, now trapped, the door firmly closed. Moving closer to the door, Tulu was aware he had severed connection with two brave young things that saved his life.

"Have a good life my dear friends, I will never forget you. If you stay with me for certain the man people will get you. Only a matter of time before they come back for me. Travel well my dear friends".

With that the old tusker ambled his way down the loading slope into the relative safety of the Zambian bush, tears streaming down his wrinkled old cheeks.

As daylight broke the full extent of the man train became clear. A group of workers were fixing boards to each of the trucks. Gradually working their way along the train. Eventually they arrived at the covered truck hiding Jango, Whisper and Benny. Along the side the man people fixed a board which advertised in bright yellow and red letters "RENDELL'S FAMILY CIRCUS". Also printed in bold black lettering across the board "NEXT STOP CATCH US IN CAPE TOWN".

South again!

# Chapter 7

"If you are tired of London, you are tired of life", wrote the English author and poet Samuel Johnson. And the same could be said for many parts of Central and Southern Africa. For once bitten by the bug that is Africa, offering many of the great wonders of the world, Africa never leaves you.

To make travel easier across its vast distances, rail links were built to provide ease of movement for humans and commercial traffic. But there was never a requirement for speed, as African trains moved at a much slower pace, crawling across the vast open spaces. Africa had never been a continent in a mad rush, it was a country with its own pace of life. The railway connecting Tanzania, Zambia, Zimbabwe,

Mozambique and South Africa was designed to move large quantities of freight. The majority towards the sea ports on the Indian Ocean: in the north, Dar es Salaam, south down the eastern seaboard to Maputo, Durban, East London and Port Elizabeth. Then on the Atlantic coast to the container port at Cape Town.

Africa's railways travelled though some of the most beautiful landscapes in the world. From the northern tip of Zimbabwe on the border with Zambia the railway crossed the Victoria Falls. Once seen, views of the 450 meter falls, known to Zimbabweans as Mosi-oa-Thunya, or "the smoke that thunders," would never be forgotten. When in full flood the columns of spray rising many metres can be seen almost 80 kilometres away. In contrast the southern section of the route ambled through South Africa calling at the Kimberly diamond mines, through the semi-desert wilderness of the Karoo, before arriving at sea level in Cape Town, the cultural centre of South Africa.

Tulu's plan was simple; for once his friends were in the safety of the large man train truck, in a short time they would be heading back north to the Serengeti close to Jango's family. Unfortunately elephants cannot read. For instead of aiming north to Nakonde on the border with Tanzania, the freight train pointed in the opposite direction. In a few short hours, Rendell's Family Circus loaded into twenty trucks would halt at the first customs post bordering Zambia and Zimbabwe, within the thunderous roar of the Victoria Falls. Tulu's heartfelt plan had gone wrong at the first move. Rather than speeding back across Zambia northwards, their destination was the southernmost tip of Africa.

Now a trio, the friends slept soundly having accepted that Tulu had no alternative but to leave them. His massive bulk would never have slotted inside the truck. For much of their new travelling home was loaded with piles of colourfully painted boxes and canvas bags, leaving just enough room for them. Furthermore, they knew travelling with Tulu would make them easy targets for the man-people. Trapped inside the man truck all they could do was wait for the door to open, then make their escape into Jango's homelands on the Serengeti.

As the train rattled along the track south from Lusaka all three gradually became accustomed to its rolling movement. On and on the train travelled closing in on their first stop. When they finally arrived at the Zambian customs post, officials from Zimbabwe would search each of the trucks before it would be allowed entry into their troubled country.

"I really need water," Jango gasped, "bound to be a water hole when we get out. This man truck can't go forever without stopping."

"Food I need food," Whisper chirped in.

Benny said nothing, what was he doing here? Just a

few days ago he lived quietly with wife and kids, moving around the woodlands with all the food they needed. Now here he was locked away in a roaring monster, no food, with two youngsters who had no idea where they were heading. Escape was his only route. Once the door opened he would be gone, zippo, out of here, he would be history.

Gradually they became aware the rolling movement was slowing, making it easier to stand without leaning against the walls for support. But their ears began to hurt from a deafening metallic screeching as the brakes were applied. In the distance man-people voices could be heard shouting orders at one another. As quickly as it started, screeching from the brakes ceased. The man train was stopping and with a huge jolt, the three of them crashed against each other.

Now their concerns changed, as they considered what danger could be waiting outside for three intrepid adventurers. Would contact with crowds of man-people spell trouble? Nervously they edged back into the corner of the large truck, terrified what they would face once the doors opened. For Tulu was no longer there to protect them, and there was no countryside in which to hide.

"Don't know about you Jango, but my plan is to run like the wind when the man people open the door. No more prisons for me, I need to be wild. You saw that I can catch my own food, I will be fine," Whisper offered.

"You can run my friend if you wish, but for me, well I'm not so fast so I'll have to take my chances," Jango replied. "What about you Benny, are you going to make a break for it?"

Benny said nothing, staring transfixed at the door, hugging a small bundle of canvas that had broken free from the boxes. Butterflies fluttered around their tummies as they thought of the possibilities of what awaited them. The voices of approaching man-people increased. Soon their door would open to begin the next stage of their adventure. For the first time since they had met, Jango watched as Whisper trembled with fear. No words were needed, the only comfort available the closeness of their bodies pressing against each other as a protection from the impending danger.

"This one next Mr Gerry if you please. No lock here, why's that sir?" the man-person questioned.

"Must have broken, you know, these things happen. Don't worry I'll get another one before we leave," Mr Gerry replied.

"Um, well what's in this one, wild animals I suppose, no need for a lock eh," another man-person cynically replied.

Inside Jango and Whisper stood back from the door as it creaked open, letting in the blinding midday sunlight from the fierce Zambian sun. Benny crouched on the boxes, his hands over his eyes, as if to "see no evil."

"No, just boxes of clothes and some of the Big Top canvas, nothing dangerous," Mr Gerry offered to the uniformed man-person. "Oh and a small bicycle, not sure who that belongs to."

"Goodbye dear friend, time for me to move on. Look after yourself and ride the two wheeler whenever you can. Remember that's your way to escape," Whisper offered to his dearest friend, tears welling in his large black eyes.

With his loudest roar, stretching to his full height, Whisper leapt from the man truck over the head of the uniformed man-person who had already dived for cover. Mr Gerry, his mouth wide open, grabbed the door for support. Petrified by his near miss with the escaping lion, the two uniformed man-people collected their clip boards, scrabbled to their feet making off from the open truck like Olympic sprinters. Whatever one of them shouted as he disappeared was out of earshot to Mr Gerry.

Jango edged to the doorway, holding his two-wheeler by his trunk. Jango had no plan to escape as he was frightened, hungry and knew that whatever he did the man-people would win. Furthermore, the step down from the man train truck was too high for him. This time there was no loading slope to assist.

Jango had already decided he had no place to go so his best choice was to be seen as a friend.

Carefully he lowered his two-wheeler, leaning it against the colourful boxes. Benny had watched as the events unfurled, understanding that escape right now held no chance of success. He was intelligent and not too dissimilar to the man-people, maybe they would get along. Aware of the plan Jango must be following, a friendly approach must surely be the way forward. Mr Gerry looked in surprise as a fully grown chimpanzee edged towards him holding a small bundle of canvas, part of Rendell Circus Big Top. Watched by Jango now confident he had chosen the way forward, Benny cautiously passed the canvas bundle to Mr Gerry as a peace offering.

"OK young man, wanna be friends?" Mr Gerry, bent forward taking the bundle.

"Yeah, good plan," Jango whispered to Benny, "still going to escape with me when the time's right?"

Benny just nodded smiling at his friend, a bonding between them had not gone unnoticed by Mr Gerry. The next part of Jango's journey would start right here, now that he was close to home. Jango would wait his time before making his escape; patience was the password to success.

But then the stark realization hit him, he had lost his two closest friends. Tulu yesterday and now his very best friend had done exactly what he promised.

There was no sign of Whisper who had taken off like the wind. The brave jungle king who could now catch his own prey, would surely survive on the outside. As he stood remembering their experiences, Jango became aware that tears were flowing down his leathery cheeks; he would probably never meet his best friend again. Their plans to meet his family gone. But what was he thinking? Whisper may have moved on, but into his life had arrived Benny. Who could tell what experiences were about to unfold with his new chimp friend.

# Chapter 8

Mustafa was not a man to suffer fools, expecting everyone to carry out his orders to the letter. He also never accepted excuses, considering excuses to be lies. Kurt had nervously sent a message telling him the bike riding elephant had escaped. Armed with the news of the loss of his prize, Mustafa screamed at the two Somalians at least twice a day for reports on their search for Jango. Whatever had happened allowing Jango to escape, Mustafa was even more determined to capture his bike riding prize.

Januna Muse and Suguli Jama the two Somalians, made no secret of the fact they were pirates, but also highly trained as jet pilots and heartless terrorists. Both men were prepared to take on any jobs, raising money for the criminal gangs for whom they worked. When Mustafa explained the money Jango's capture could bring, at first they laughed, but soon realised this could be one of the biggest ransoms they had dealt with.

After Jango and Whisper had escaped across the Ikuu River, Januna and Suguli had tried to follow them, even employing a Masai guide, but with no success. There was no alternative but to wait for more information that would certainly come to them from a network of contacts throughout Africa.

"Well, well, well, what do we have here then?" Mr Gerry questioned. "You're a very fine young fella, about two years I'd think. Judy, come and see what I've found."

Jango stood his ground watching as the audience grew. This was becoming like his days performing for the man- people outside the gates of the Nursery. Maybe this was how he could escape. It was all so similar, but he had no Whisper or Hutch to help plan his getaway.

"Of course, the two-wheeler that's the way. Let the man-people have their fun watching me go through my tricks, then back to freedom," Jango mused. But would Benny fit into his escape plan?

"And look here Judy, another prize, what shall we call him, maybe Chipper the Chimp, yeah that'll be good."

Jango started to giggle, "Chipper the Chimp, now I like that, very smart name for a monkey."

"You wait till he finds a name for you, what about Shorty or Stumpy," Benny retorted.

"Judy, I'm sure they're talking to each other, and I'm sure they understand us, always have you know," Mr Gerry offered his hand to Benny who moved closer to the friendly man-people.

Nearby man-people began screaming accompanied by a roar that Jango would recognise anywhere. From under another nearby truck his best friend appeared, scattering man-people in every direction. But Mr Gerry and Judy stood firm, leaning against the man truck, Judy stroking Jango, Mr Gerry holding Benny, each frozen to the spot. For they understood once a lion intended to attack, it would be curtains for them both. Placing each foot as though treading on rice paper, Whisper tentatively approached Jango. His gleaming white teeth bared as an act of defiance, as he closed towards his friend and the two man-people.

"Did you think I'd leave you my tusker friend?" Whisper shouted out to his friend. "By the way, did you see how many man-people ran from this great lion king? Did these man-people hurt you Jango, I can chase them off you know?"

Mr Gerry and Judy stood fixed to the spot, certain the young lion had only interest in the welfare of his friends, and would not attack them.

"Don't move Judy, I think they're talking to each other, just like these two. I think the young lion came back to help his friend. And do you know what; I think these young fellas want to stay with us."

"Whisper, please go before the man-people come back with their stick that shouts, then you'll never get back to the wild. Please my dear friend, I've got a plan. You remember the Nursery how they fell for my two-wheeler tricks? Well, when I'm ready I'll do the same again. Now scram and get away safely my friend," Jango pleaded.

In the distance the sound of man-people machines rumbled closer. Soon Whisper would have no way to escape.

"Go my friend, don't let them catch you," Jango pleaded again.

"Please you stupid beast go, I'll look after him, now run," Benny ordered.

Reluctantly Whisper turned towards the approaching man machines, understanding that it must be now or feel the dart that makes you sleep pierce his skin.

"OK, but I'll come back for you Jango, you're my only family," Whisper shouted as he turned away.

With that the graceful beast returned under the

nearby truck making his way towards the roaring Victoria Falls. As Whisper disappeared, both Mr Gerry and Judy were unsure why the young lion had not attacked them. Through the whole event Mr Gerry stood silently softly rubbing Jango's ear, whilst holding on to Benny. Mr Gerry was totally convinced the young lion was only interested in the welfare of his travelling companions. A closeness had been shown between wild animals that few could ever understand. The young lion now on a quest for safety in the great expanses of the African bush. The young tusker and his chimpanzee friend seeking something entirely different, maybe an escape plan.

Clouds of dust swamped over the truck as the two man machines screeched to a halt. Several man-people with guns jumped out from either side of the machine. As the dust settled the man-people began searching for Whisper, but the graceful beast had long since disappeared. With the lion scare over, all that remained was a young tusker standing in the doorway of the man train truck. His travelling companion standing quietly beside Mr Gerry, the two still holding hands.

One of the uniformed man-people who had run when Whisper leapt over him, made his way to Mr Gerry and Judy. Nervously he approached, looking around for any sign of further danger. This man-person could stop Rendell's Circus moving into Zimbabwe, then on to Cape Town.

"Go, get out of here and take those beasts with you," he ordered thrusting an envelope into Mr Gerry's hand. "And lock them up or next time I'll have them shot if I see them again." Grabbing the customs papers Mr Gerry smiled at Jango, easing him back into truck.

"Well done old son, now let's get you some food, I guess you'll be starving. When we get to Hwange our next stop, we'll get you out of here to stretch your legs."

Jango felt comfortable around these man-people. Mr Gerry seems to be a good man and Judy also seemed to be kind. Another man-person approached carrying two large buckets. One filled with fruit, the other water. Jango's was in heaven, no need to scavenge in the bush when food and water is brought to him.

"Judy seen this before?" queried Mr Gerry holding up Jango's two-wheeler, "new to me, must have been left by those Italian tightrope walkers."

Jango had carried and ridden his two wheeler many miles and no one was taking it away from him now. Stretching out his trunk he eased it away from Mr Gerry, hugging it against his legs.

"Wow, big fella, if you want the bike it's yours," Mr Gerry smiled. "Haven't seen a tusker ride a bike before. First for everything young fella, relax!"

Jango smiled to himself knowing his trick riding would be his way to escape, especially using the kindness of Mr Gerry. As he munched away at the bucket of fruit he couldn't stop thinking of his friend Whisper. They had faced many dangerous situations, probably saved Tulu's life, whilst travelling across Tanzania and Zambia. But Whisper had changed. Once he'd learned to roar he had convinced himself he had become king of the jungle. They had laughed together at their mutual attempts to play grownups. Their friendship coupled with youthful exuberance had seen them through many difficulties. Life had to go on and soon they would get their chance to escape.

Still Jango had no idea he was heading 180 degrees in the wrong direction. For Cape Town at the southernmost tip of Africa was the destination of Rendell's Circus, not Kenya in the north.

With a bang the door slammed shut. This time only the bottom half of the door was secured, the top half pinned back allowing Jango and Benny an excellent view of the passing countryside. Leaning against the door Jango stared in disbelief as the roar of the Victoria Falls challenged the rattle from the man train. He had seen clouds over the escarpment near his home, but never anything like the billowing spray rising from the thundering falls. Eventually the noise from Victoria Falls faded into the background allowing the rattle of the man train to take over.

The bush sped past and across the open plains. Jango had an uninterrupted view. Across the never ending bush were gangling giraffes, herds of ambling zebra, groups of impalas leaping like spring lambs and several families of ostriches scratching for food. On and on went the man train through the open bush, the two friends grateful for the half opened door allowing fresh air to rush in as they sped farther south.

Jango was soon bored with the countryside which appeared endless, eventually causing him to settle down and doze off rocked by the gentle movement of the man train.

"Come on little fella, rise and shine, time for a stroll," Mr Gerry called peering over the door with two other man-people. "Ok boys, he'll be no trouble although I think we should put two ropes on him, but don't frighten him."

As Jango woke from a deep sleep he could see the doors were now fully open, Mr Gerry standing next to him with another bucket of water. Very gently, so not to frighten Jango, Mr Gerry placed a rope around his neck, tying it loosely. Each of the man-people now standing in the man truck looked surprised as Jango standing with a rope lead, appeared to smile at each in turn.

"Come on little fella, let's take you for a stroll," he offered, taking Benny by the hand.

Jango resisted stopping by his two-wheeler. Wrapping his trunk around the handlebars he pulled it along with him. When he reached the doorway the drop to the ground had disappeared. Just like the place they had climbed in when Tulu had helped them; Jango could step out onto a raised platform. Mr Gerry proud of his control over Jango, with Benny also walking like a toddler, eased them both onto the ramp to be greeted by cheers from a number of man-people.

"I'll play along with the man-people, I'll show them my two-wheeler tricks and then off into the distance," Jango offered to Benny. "Mamma and papa here I come."

Standing outside the truck Jango could see a slope leading down, an ideal place to show his talents. Mr Gerry had let the rope stay long and loose. Enough for Jango make it away on his two-wheeler, beginning to scoot down the ramp. His timing was perfect as Mr Gerry looked away shouting for Judy to join them to watch their new friend.

 One foot on the pedal, the other shoving with all his might, Jango scooted away. The rope tightened slightly before it slid from Mr Gerry's hand. As his speed increased Jango threw his leg over the saddle settling himself into a full riding position. Hitting the bottom of the slope Jango pushed the pedals to gain speed, the rope now dragging behind.

All the man-people looked on, shocked at the young tusker racing away from them on a small rusty bicycle. For there, performing in front of them was probably the most exciting circus act they had ever witnessed. Jango now fifty metres away scampered on, unaware he was in a sealed compound from where there was virtually no exit, no escape.

As Jango made greater distance from the man-people the sudden realization hit the gathered spectators that Jango could be escaping. Several jumped into the waiting man machines to chase after him, still pedalling at least two hundred metres away. Mr Gerry unlike the others chasing after Jango, stood motionless smiling at the unfolding events. He'd stopped in this railway yard at Hwange many times, fully aware there was no escape. The track was secured by heavy gates, only opened when security guards allowed authorised trains to pass through.

Jango was now moving smoothly, but in the distance he'd already spotted the security gates blocking his escape. Jango realised to make a perfect escape he must gain the total trust of the man-people. Back at the Nursery, Jango had mastered many tricks, turning in a circle, the most vital aspect of riding the two-wheeler. More advanced tricks could follow. For now was the perfect time to gain Mr Gerry's trust.

Turning to his right Jango changed direction in a large semi-circle, aiming his two-wheeler back towards the loading ramp. Hurrying towards him, the man machines slowed to a walking pace. It was time to have some fun with the man-people. Jango began weaving from side to side as he cycled between the two man machines, aiming gracefully back towards the waiting figure of Mr Gerry. As though returning from a Sunday leisurely bike ride in the countryside, Jango dismounted, before pushing his two-wheeler back up the ramp. Reaching the open door, he turned and dipped his trunk in salute to Mr Gerry, before getting himself and his two wheeler into the truck. The first part of his plan to escape had been won. Now he must fight on, work with the man-people, then next time leave for good.

# Chapter 9

The stop at Hwange was enforced by the need of the Rendell train to take on water and coal. Whatever the time of year this was never a favourite stopping place for Rendell's Circus. For Hwange was one of the largest open cast coal mines in Africa. The smells coming from the coal workings leaving a taste floating in the air that no one enjoyed. Fortunately, as this was only a stopover for fuel, it was only scheduled to be a few hours.

In the yard where the circus train stopped, were several other freight trains laden with coal and coke to be transported to sea ports along the coast in South Africa and Mozambique. Overlooking the freight yard stood an ancient two storey office building, most of the windows stained from exposure to the coal dust.

Klaus Binderfeld had been a regular visitor to Hwange for many years. His company bought coal and coke, shipping it to wherever he could get the best price. Today as he sat discussing his next coal deal in the offices, screams of excitement could be heard from outside in the freight yard. Everyone ran to the windows overlooking the parked trains, their attention drawn to Jango as he performed on his two-wheeler.

Jango's talents were now an open secret. Unlike the information Kurt had relayed to Mustafa which would be held secret, here was a public display of one of Rendell Circus animals performing for all to see. Klaus eased his way closer to the window, like the other office workers, disbelieving the extraordinary performance taking place in the freight yard, alongside the Rendell train.

"But I'm telling you, your highness, I've been watching a baby elephant riding a bicycle in the freight yard here in Hwange. Yes of course your next train is loaded, your highness. But the elephant is worth twice what we can get for the coal. Yes sir, I promise." Klaus forced the news to his Royal partner.

Through the window Klaus could see the crowd increasing, many having joined from the offices.

Jango was now back at the top of the ramp enjoying the cheers and waving to the gathering. Benny, not to be out done, settled on Jango's back, riding him like a jockey, now part of the act.

Klaus replaced the telephone receiver then sat back looking at the crowds, understanding just what he had to do. There was no rush, for Rendells would promote this amazing young elephant as their latest act, attracting interest from around the world. Then would be the time to take the young elephant and sell him to his Royal partner or maybe one of many contacts.

# Chapter 10

For the next two days they continued on their journey south. Again they halted at a customs post, this time to leave Zimbabwe at Beitbridge into South Africa. On this occasion there were no frenzied scenes with lions leaping to escape, no customs officers running for their lives. As the train waited to cross into South Africa armed customs guards took a cursory glance at the trucks containing Rendell's Circus, only too happy for it to move on without a full inspection.

Stories had passed quickly down the line of the crazed lion jumping over the head of the captain of the guard, a sufficient deterrent. Jango watched with interest as uniformed man-people wandered around carrying tranquiliser guns. But within the confines of his truck Jango didn't feel that these man-people posed any threat to them. Eventually he heard the sounds similar to those that stopped his escape back at Victoria Falls.

Jango and Benny now had a chance to view another great river as they crossed the bridge into South Africa. The Limpopo flowed into the distance from their viewpoint in the truck. Below they could see a number of Hutch's relatives, wallowing around the river's edge. A herd of water buffalo grazing on the grass spreading along the river bank. None of the animals showing any interest as Rendell's train rattled past and into the distance.

Exhausted from the boredom of being locked in the rattling truck, Jango flopped down sleeping for several hours. When he awoke it was pitch black, but their trucks continued their seemingly endless journey. Daylight brought yet more non-ending wilderness as they meandered their way through the Karoo.

Jango and Benny had now travelled many hours in the company of unopened boxes, which took over half their truck. For who could tell what treasures they held? Hopefully food, a few buckets of apples or a bale of hay would satisfy their everlasting hunger. Elephants teeth are not the sharpest in the world: so chewing the string tying the boxes was a non-starter. But Jango had a formidable tool: Benny. His plan was simple; he would sit on each of the boxes, whilst Benny ripped them open. Several were canvas bags which Benny considered should be his first target. Immediately suffering Jango's weight, the first two canvas bags burst open with a tearing sound, requiring no need for Benny's dexterous fingers.

Like mischievous school children they scrabbled into the broken boxes. Delving into the possible treasures they had uncovered. More boxes and bags were forced open but not a sign of anything edible, what use would gaudy dresses and clown outfits be for them? Their attempts to find food a disaster, their truck now a litter box scattered with torn circus clothing.

# Chapter 11

Brigit strode around the training ground oblivious to the activities being performed simultaneously all around her by different members of the circus troupe. Her trunk swishing dust clouds across her back in an attempt to flush the irritating birds, seeking a free ride whilst searching for flies resting on her wrinkled hide.

Within the fenced training pen, six brilliant white stallions, in full show-time regalia pranced elegantly in a synchronized step formation close by her. Not a step out of place, each hoof pounding the dusty training ring as one. Standing across the front two stallions, Franco the trick riding specialist, casually dressed in jeans and a New York Yankees tee-shirt, worked through his act. Over and over he went taking the team of thrusting stallions through turns and various changes of step.

Brigit had seen Franco lookalikes come and go during her years as one of the star turns of Rendell's Circus. For like any seasoned performer she respected other acts. But these days it failed to bolster real enthusiasm, taking little more than a cursory glance, however brilliant the acts may be. She'd seen them all. Lion tamers, an idiot shoving his head into a tiger's mouth, teams of performing dogs, even a hippo who could run in circles for a few rounds of the ring, carrying the aging ringmaster who insisted on singing.

Each day Brigit would run through her tricks in the training grounds, sitting, kneeling and bowing to an imaginary audience. Then her finale, swinging Gerry Rendell, Mr Gerry to most of the performers, across her neck where he would take his bow, blowing kisses to an appreciative crowd. She could perform her act blind fold with one leg tied behind her back, but somehow she was not really content. Her life was comfortable and uncomplicated, for she was fed, loved by her keepers and adored by a changing cast of spectators.

Brigit had travelled across Africa and parts of Europe with Mr Gerry but she had been left out of this latest trip. In fact just a small troupe was taken on this last tour, leaving all the horses, lions and two nasty tempered brown bears at home. Brigit missed the smell of the circus and the noise from the audience as they screamed in delight at a cast of talented performers.

Left behind at base camp just north of Cape Town, Brigit had been given a new task. Before he left for the current tour, Mr Gerry had introduced her to a two year old elephant called Jessica. Jessica was an orphan who had shown a natural talent to work with the circus folk, joining Brigit's training in the practice rings. As the weeks passed Jessica mastered the act. She tied her trunk to Brigit's tail as they eventually increased their pace circling the ring. Her final trick to stop and turn through 360 degrees, maybe three or four times, that's if she remembered. Brigit quickly grew to love the baby she had never had, happy to become Jessica's surrogate mother.

Whilst Mr Gerry was touring with the smaller circus, rehearsals never stopped for the other performers. For many new acts had arrived, keen to be given an audition in front of Mr Gerry and his wife Judy. Jessica would not have to perform an audition, as with Brigit she had already shown her natural talent, giving Brigit's act just the little freshness it needed.

Rendell's Circus had been performing throughout Southern and Central Africa for over fifty years. Started by Mr Gerry Rendell's father Archie in 1963, when together with friends who performed for food money along the waterfront in Cape Town, they decided to form a circus troupe. Archie Rendell was an accomplished juggler, performing with knives, fire sticks and sometimes chain saws. Together with tightrope walkers, clowns and a changing cast of gymnasts, they had sufficient talent to perform their own open air show.

Archie's big chance came in 1964 when a rich gold trader from Johannesburg, bored with his day to day business, decided that investing in a circus was his needed escape. Now free from the tedium of the cut and thrust of business he lost himself in a world of clowns, performing animals and endless pretty girls. As the years passed, Rendell's circus became the byword for top class circus entertainment throughout Africa. Lords, ladies, kings, presidents and famous personalities from the movies visited Archie's famous circus.

On reaching his seventieth birthday, Archie now riddled with arthritis, had accepted that even the simplest movement had become difficult. So he reluctantly handed the reins of the circus to his eldest son Mr Gerry. Mr Gerry like many born into a circus family had not shown great interest in his studies, skipping school whenever the circus went on tour. Mr Gerry showed early on his love for training animals. Many considering he established a closer affinity to his animals than with the human members of the circus. However, Mr Gerry was a taskmaster, determined to expand the international appeal of the circus, not only throughout Africa, but to expand his family's circus to Europe and beyond. Over the past few years Mr Gerry had developed two distinct circuses. The traditional Big Top Circus, following the well trodden path with clowns, animal acts, and a wide selection of acrobatic and trapeze acts. This coupled to a small zoo where his audiences could get close to his precious animals.

Financial problems were killing off the traditional family circus businesses. Mr Gerry's new circus was going to be cheaper to stage meaning the survival of the Rendell family as a circus. There were no animals and the series of unique acrobatic acts from across the globe, choreographed to modern music encouraged a changing modern audience. There were also pressures from many outsiders suggesting circus animals were badly treated. Their opinions were complete nonsense, for practically all Rendell's circus animals led secure and happy lives, most having no wish to return to the wild.

Apart from Brigit, for she could no longer remember living in the wild, and longed to explore an existence away from the confines of the circus. Mr Gerry had trained Brigit taking responsibility for all her needs, since the day she entered the circus some twenty years ago. They had formed a bond that made life easy for Mr Gerry as her trainer.

Mr Archie, as Mr Gerry's father was affectionately known, had saved Brigit from the Etosha National Park in the far north of Namibia. Brigit had been deserted by her mother when they were separated during a raging bush fire, when no more than six years old. Baby elephants stay close to their mothers for several years and Brigit was no exception, the only hope being an elephant orphanage. Sadly the structure of the Etosha Park could only care for a small number of young orphans. The Park's problem was Mr Archie's good fortune. He immediately shipped the young elephant to the Rendell training camp near Cape Town.

Brigit thrived on the love and care shown by everyone and soon became the star turn of the circus. Life was so good that Brigit wandered free, being tethered only during the hours of darkness for her own safety. As the years progressed Brigit led the procession anytime the circus swept into a new town, always seeing herself as the prima donna.

Frequently she would play to the gathered crowds spraying water over the expectant children. Over time Brigit realized as an old circus hand, every act needed to evolve and improvements made. The inclusion of Jessica had without a doubt changed their act. Although, early on Jessica was limited to being towed by Brigit's tail and occasionally when she remembered the routine, a few complete rotations. Now something else was needed to ensure the cheers kept ringing out at every performance.

Several years ago Mr Archie had convinced the South African Rail Company that running a train line into his training camp would have many advantages for all concerned. Mr Archie was a fervent believer in rail transport and where possible planned the circus tours using the rail system. Not only was the train line into the Rendell camp used to move the circus around, tour company's also ran trips to view the Rendell zoo and watch rehearsals. In fact Rendells' had become a small township, one of the larger employers in the Northern Cape.

# Chapter 12

The clanging of the Rendell train broke the concentration of everyone rehearsing in the various open air rings and rigging scattered around the practice ground. For the tour had arrived home, all twenty railway trucks, some covered wagons, some open to the elements, rattled to a halt. Immediately all rehearsals stopped, to a man everyone around the camp made their way to the arriving train, eager for the Rendell Circus family to be reunited. Brigit with Jessica in tow ambled towards the gathering crowds, keen to see if any new surprises would discharge from the long man train.

From the first of the passenger carriages, Mr Gerry and Judy climbed down to be greeted by everyone, all enthusiastic for news of the tour. Mr Gerry although ready for news from the training camp had other thoughts; Judy already aware what would be his first port of call. Slowly he made his way through the noisy throng, smiling gratefully and shaking hands with a number of his friends, aiming towards his target. There she was, Brigit his very favourite, leading Jessica as though bringing her forward for an audience.

"Have I got a surprise for you my girl, just what we've been searching for. Come on my friend," Mr Gerry affectionately held her ear, leading her gently towards one of the trucks.

As they approached the truck, Jango's trunk was hanging over the bottom door, peering out at the gathered throng of man-people. Benny had already found a defensive position offering a perfect view, squatting on Jango's neck, uncertain what to expect.

"Holy moly Mr Jango my man! What have we got here? More man-people than I've ever seen!" Benny offered, cowering lower on Jango's neck.

"It'll be fine my friend, remember our plan, make friends and when the time's right, we're out of here, back to the bush," Jango confirmed.

"Benny look, the good man-people and two elephants. One's my age I think. Benny! They're both girls, what do think of that?" he continued as Brigit, Jessica and Mr Gerry approached their truck.

"Well young tusker, brought some friends for you, let's get you out of there," Mr Gerry unbolted the door allowing it to swing open.

Standing for the gathered masses Jango peered into the crowd, casually leaning against his two-wheeler. Benny determined to keep his position was still perched on Jango's neck. Behind the adult elephant and the youngster, a man machine closed towards them with a device they pushed against the truck, offering Jango and Benny a route to ground level. Mr Gerry made his way up the ramp and stroked Jango tenderly on his trunk with one hand, also offering comfort with his other hand to Benny.

"OK my beauties, welcome to my home!" Mr Gerry smiled at the two friends. "I promise you'll have fun here and Brigit will look after you," he offered pointing at Brigit, who was looking bemused at this strange situation.

Benny, still uncertain about the world he'd arrived in, decided Mr Gerry must be his ally, for he had already shown him continuing kindness. Jango could see a further chance to show the gathered man-people how talented he had become. Maybe a little out of practice, but as his father always told him, if you fall, jump on again and pedal like mad.

So here was another chance to show the world. Mr

Gerry, fully aware of the little tuskers' talent, smiled at Jango, nodding his head in the direction of the ramp. The crowd fell silent as Jango moved into position; his left foot on the left hand pedal, ready to scoot down the ramp, now firmly attached to their truck. Man-people who had been standing near the bottom edged away leaving a clear pathway away from the ramp.

"Jango my tusker friend, you show them! Go for it!" Benny yelled.

Mr Gerry was again convinced the two friends were chatting away to each other.

"Hi ho! And here we go, see you soon Benny."

With that, down the ramp Jango dashed, steering his rusting two-wheeler between the crowds of stunned circus man-people. To begin with there was no sound other than the clatter of the two-wheeler as it rushed down the metal ramp. As Jango gained speed the man-people looked on in disbelief, no one more shocked than the two elephants.

Brigit had heard of other animals riding two-wheelers. She remembered an Alsatian dog and two monkeys at a circus where she had been to perform by Mr Gerry. But an elephant! This was almost beyond belief. Jango hit the dusty training ground, in full control pedalling at an increasing speed, now waving his trunk at the crowds. In return the man-people were cheering wildly as Jango passed between them.

Mr Gerry sidled up to Brigit, both having already worked out how their best-selling act would change. Mr Gerry could already see two young elephants, one riding a two-wheeler, the other performing simpler tricks. All that with Brigit's proven repertoire, they would be the best circus act ever. Thousands would come to see the famous Rendell elephant trio. They would travel to countries far and wide entertaining audiences screaming in delight watching a young elephant riding his two-wheeler. Together with Brigit and Jessica, Mr Gerry led them all through the crowds to where Jango had tumbled off, having crashed into one of the practice rings.

"That showed them young tusker," Benny hollered, holding Mr Gerry's hand as they approached him. "Now how do we escape, Jango, too many man-people for my liking," he continued.

"It'll come Benny, just got to wait, the right opportunity will come, trust me, I've already escaped once," Jango insisted.

"Yeah, but you got caught again, that's why we're here, maybe I should work out the plan," Benny insisted.

"Well well, young man, that's quite a trick, where on earth did you learn that?" Brigit moved closer to Jango, Jessica moving even closer to Brigit, uncertain if the two-wheeler could harm her.

"My brother I guess, he's a very good rider, then papa showed me how to balance without the stabilizers. My name's Jango and my best friend is Benny," Jango offered.

"Oh I forgot my manners, I'm Brigit and my young friend is Jessica. So where did they catch you? You're lucky that Mr Gerry found you, he's a wonderful man," Brigit continued.

Since he was a child working with animals, Mr Gerry was always convinced that animals spoke to each other. Maybe some spoke different languages, even dialects, but then again so did humans. He longed to talk to the animals, just like the story of Dr John Doolittle, who understood many different animals that he treated as a vet. If only Mr Gerry could communicate with these wonderful creatures that he loved so much, he could be honest with them. For changes were about to happen to the famous Rendell's Circus.

Rendell's was a business not a charity. After several family meetings the decision was made to close the traditional Big Top Circus and concentrate on a modern form of circus which was more theatre than circus. In three months' time that last traditional Rendell's Family Circus would perform in the Big Top which would be erected at the Rendell training camp. This was where Archie Rendell started and this was where the last Big Top Circus would perform.

The biggest decision for Mr Gerry and his father; how to deal with the disposal of all fourteen of their talented performing animals, plus twenty other animals that made up their small but popular zoo. There was nowhere for them to go. No longer could they trade them to another circus, for others would be dealing with exactly the same issues. Their only alternative was to sell their beloved animals to a number of selected zoos around the world.

Brigit his favourite could no longer be considered young, although she was the best and most reliable performer at Rendells. However, there were several months before the final decision had to be made and although Mr Gerry was Mr Circus, as a businessman he lacked the same talent. Right now he wanted to bring Jango into the act with Brigit and Jessica. There were another sixty performances of the Rendell's Big Top and Mr Gerry would make sure that his circus would be the talk of the circus world. Rendell's Big Top would finish with a bang.

Whatever their concerns regarding dangers posed by man-people, from what they had already seen, life at Rendell's was safe and comfortable. Brigit had immediately shown Jango the ropes. Although Jango insisted that he came as a package with Benny, Brigit was suspicious of Benny, as with the other chimpanzees she'd met.

Brigit had instantly accepted that Jango's talents would bring that extra sparkle missing from her act.

Moreover, Jango must feel free to express himself. Already their rehearsals collected increasing crowds every time the new group tried out their new act in the practice rings. Benny was their eyes and ears, a role together with Jango he had secretly developed. His task was simple; to watch for any ways they could escape, any way they could return home: Jango back to his parents on the Serengeti and Benny back to wife and his kids, although he was certain the kids would have grown and left their mother.

# Chapter 13

As the weeks went by the Elephant Trio as they were now billed, attracted rave notices from local TV news stations, which soon went global. Articles appeared in glossy magazines all over the world showing the baby elephant who could ride a two-wheeled bike. The Elephant Trio were stars, everyday more and more reporters visited the camp. Everyday their act improved, Brigit the centre piece, Jessica now advanced to standing on her front or back legs as well as her spinning top routine. But a fourth dimension had been added; Benny had joined the act riding on Jango's back and leaping through rings. The Elephant Trio had now become the Rendell Four.

However, the star turn was always going to be Jango. He would arrive to dimmed lights, a trumpet fanfare, then to belting rock anthems as he cycled his newly painted two-wheeler round the Big Top. Following a standing ovation Jango would then commence his party tricks. He would leap across from one side of the trusty two-wheeler to the other, then perch on the handlebars, facing forward. Then with Benny's assistance he would sit on the handlebars facing backwards. His finale would be performed with Brigit. Benny holding on to Jango's spangled collar waving at the crowd, at the last minute Brigit would rear up on her back legs, Jango speeding under, the two slapping trunks as they passed.

The applause was deafening, as all four took their bows to a rousing rendition of Queen belting out "We are the Champions". Never in the history of Big Top circus had Mr Archie or Mr Gerry heard such a response from a circus crowd.

# Chapter 14

Sheik Mohamed bounced his son Prince Halim on his knee, as they watched the massive TV screen showing a Sky News report on the new circus sensation performing at Rendell's Circus in Cape Town.

"You should see this my dear," the Sheik called to his wife Princess Leila to join them. "This is exactly what we need for Halim's new zoo. We've got two lions, water buffalo and others joining us, but a bicycle riding elephant, what a triumph that would be my dear. Think of the honour of having such a creature."

"So I shall go to meet these Rendell people and

acquire the beast," Princess Leila arrogantly butted in. "How much shall I pay my dear, do you think fifty thousand dollars?"

"We shall make no mistakes, yes of course you will attempt to buy the beast, more if you must but just in case I shall arrange for Colonel Ahmed to join you there to remove the creature safely and return it here." the Sheik continued. "I shall instruct him today. It will take a few days for him to asemble his team, so you should leave tomorrow and meet with these Rendell people."

Sheik Mohamed was not a patient man feeling that his enormous wealth could buy whatever and whoever he wanted, anytime he wanted. His plan to instruct the merciless mercenary Colonel Ahmed showed he meant to capture Jango for Prince Halim, whatever the cost.

In Oman, Sheik Mohamed was planning to openly acquire Jango, with a backup plan now being worked through with Colonel Ahmed as a military exercise to ensure capturing Jango for his son, if Princess Leila failed.

Sheik Mohamed had access to first class research and military planning at his fingertips. His meeting with Colonel Ahmed was brief and to the point: Use whatever military and civilian facilities needed to bring the bike riding elephant home for his son.

In contrast the news about the elephant that had

escaped from the Nursery had filtered back to Mustafa through series of paid informers. Most being unsavoury characters who were paid for information and desperate to keep on the good side of the old Arab. Mustafa could be generous if he got what he wanted, but equally unkind to those who failed him or supplied incorrect information.

Within Rendell's training camp two of the security guards formed part of Mustafa's network. Supplying information, most seeming unimportant to the old Arab, could earn them a few extra Rand. The arrival of Jango on the Rendell train was just such information the security men should pass on to the old Arab. Although they had no idea the interest Mustafa had in the bike riding elephant, both deemed it vital the knowledge of the performing elephant should be supplied to Mustafa. Immediately Mustafa contacted his two Somalians relaying the exciting news. Within hours the Somalians had begun to devise a plan to ensure the performing beast would be theirs.

Unlike Mustafa, Klaus Binderfeld already had the latest information, with contacts travelling on the circus train. His information updated twice daily on the location of Jango and the plans Gerry Rendell had for the performing elephant. Klaus knew that he would not be the only one prepared to take the little gold mine away from the Rendells. He was a patient man and quite prepared for someone else to make the first move. To Klaus this was a game of chess, his move to check mate would be imminent. Although his Royal colleague had shown indifference when they discussed the performing elephant, there was a certainty he would pay to have such a prize under his control.

# Chapter 15

As with all good things, they must come to an end. Although there was a waiting list for tickets for the remaining shows, deep down there was sadness surrounding all the Rendell family. They were aware of the hard financial facts of life that would see all their beloved animals sold to various zoos. As the day for the last show drew nearer, Mr Archie noticed his son had become withdrawn; spending much of his time sitting with Jango, Brigit, Jessica, with Benny perched on his knee.

"I can't send you guys to London Zoo, it would be like a prison, but what can I do?" Mr Gerry muttered to himself sitting on hay bales outside the building kept as the group's night-time shelter.

Mr Gerry never heard the crunch of gravel under the tyres of the black stretched limousine as it edged its way to the building. A grey uniformed chauffeur hopped smartly to open the rear doors. He bowed slightly as a tall beautiful lady, her hair covered with a black silk scarf stepped elegantly from the limo.

"Mr Gerry Rendell?" the lady asked, "I'm Princess Leila, wife of Sheik Mohamed from Oman, I would like to speak with you about one of your elephants," she continued moving close to him, aware he was not interested in her presence.

"I'm sorry, excuse me," Mr Gerry stood, waking from his thoughts to greet her. "They're all sold ma'am to the London Zoo; you can see them at their new home later this year."

"You don't understand Mr Rendell, Sheik Mohamed has already built a spectacular new open plan zoo which is over 500 acres and has every luxury for our animals."

"I don't understand, what's that got to do with us?" Mr Gerry was already becoming uncomfortable with the conversation.

"We will buy the two small elephants for a very good price, I think fifty thousand US dollars is acceptable, yes?" Princess Leila interrupted.

"But Princess Leila please understand, they're already sold. You're very welcome to watch them at the final show tomorrow, but after that I'm afraid they'll be leaving us."

"Mr Rendell, my husband has decided that your two young elephants will be our star turn, the price is unimportant, if he wants them he will have them. I suggest you prepare them for travel. My people will be in touch, good day Mr Rendell," with that she left leaving a large brown envelope on the hay bales next to Mr Gerry.

With a swirl of expensive silk she was back inside the stretched limo, which took off spreading choking dust clouds over Mr Gerry and his beloved friends.

"What do you make of that?" Jango challenged his friends. "First we're off to some place called London Zoo, next our man person tells the Princess we're not for sale. All very complicated, but I still want to get home to mamma and papa."

As her limo sped away from Rendell's camp, Princess Leila was still seething at Mr Gerry rejection of her offer. She's a Princess and her husband's money can buy anything. How dare he reject her? Angrily she stabbed out a series of numbers on the limo's phone system. Princess Leila was aware her failure must be reported to her husband, who would be decidedly unimpressed. Securing the young elephant as their son's latest plaything was her mission, failure not an option. For several minutes she listened as new orders were delivered by the Sheik.

Given no chance for niceties the phone call was terminated, her hands still shaking with anger. She had one more chance to make amends, she had to have those elephants for her spoilt son. She would succeed, failure was not an option. Even as the Sheik's number one wife she would never be forgiven if she did not secure Jango.

Her limo turned into an ex-military airport gliding to a halt alongside a massive Airbus A400M Military Transport aircraft. Her arrival alerted a group of men in beige military combats standing by the ramp. As the limo halted they stood to attention awaiting the presence of Princess Leila, now wearing similar attire to her men; she had piled her long black hair under a black baseball cap. Like clockwork they formed a guard around her, leading her back into the rear of the Airbus.

Carefully Princess Leila made an inspection of the equipment readied for their task. These including a 10 ton Mercedes flatbed truck with a crane attached, resting on a steel cage, destined to be Jango's temporary home. Behind the flatbed truck, two Land Rovers, one an open pick up and the other a hard top with a look out panel removed from the roof. She had a well organised team, fully equipped and armed ready for action. It was clear this team of mercenaries had been well funded by her husband and supplied with unmarked equipment. As Princess

Leila made her way to the front of the aircraft, Colonel Ahmed invited her to sit with him. For several minutes they were deep in conversation. Eventually the Colonel stood and saluted Princess Leila as she left for her waiting limo.

Across the airfield, parked close to the runway was a black Gulf Stream G200, its engines running, ready for an immediate take off. Without waiting for any formalities Princess Leila and her staff boarded the aircraft, the doors closed and the Gulf Stream's nose pointed towards the runway.

# Chapter 16

From the confines of their shelter Jango and his friends heard the excited sounds of the crowds making their way into the Big Top and the circus band in full swing, playing a selection of traditional circus music. The atmosphere was building up in the Big Top. TV crews searched amongst the crowds for interesting people to interview, turning the most improbable comments into meaningful sound bites.

Merchandisers were already fast selling out of Jango T shirts, Brigit baseball caps and a bizarre pink tutu with Jessica's image stencilled front and back. But the biggest hot-sell of the day was the flag emblazoned with a picture of the smiling Rendell Four.

Even with the Four as top billing there was no question where the media spotlight was focused. Jango the bike riding elephant had been in magazines the world over and details of his talent being downloaded on endless web sites. Mr Gerry and Mr Archie were simple circus people, so the thought of making vast fortunes selling Jango's marketing rights across the world, was to them anathema.

Mr Gerry and his father continued busying themselves carrying out their duties front of house. Mixing with dignitaries and special needs children, ensuring the front row seats for this final performance were made available. After tonight's performance Rendell's Circus would take on a completely different format. Furthermore, they would no longer be dogged by hordes do-gooders complaining about the treatment of their beloved animals. Mr Gerry had smiled at everyone, before making his way through security to be with his precious friends for their final performance in his Big Top.

The shelter which had served as home for Jango, Brigit, Jessica and Benny, was luxury itself. Everything had been considered by Mr Gerry when it was constructed. Two pairs of swing doors secured the building; full height solid metal doors. Then inside lower gates, allowing the occupants light with full visibility of the adjoining practice grounds. During the day, both sets of gates were left wide open, allowing the friends freedom throughout the compound. Although they understood this evening was to be the last performance, their future was decidedly unclear. London Zoo was the name bandied about. Each one of them loved Mr Gerry and the other man-people who worked with him. Together they had developed an act that had changed the appeal of Big Top circus, so the reason for this change saddened them and tomorrow their fate would hopefully become clear.

"And now my Lords, ladies and gentlemen, the act you've all been waiting for," Mr Archie bellowed, "I think I can say, the world famous, the one and only Rendell Four."

With a theatrical wave of his arms, pointing towards the curtained entrance, Mr Archie moved towards the rope retaining the curtains to welcome the arrival of the final act. Over the sound system more Queen music, this time "We will rock you", which encouraged synchronized clapping from the packed audience. With a further dramatic gesture Mr Archie tugged the rope releasing the scarlet and gold curtains. The howl from the crowd swallowed Freddie Mercury's vocals. But there was no sight of the Rendell Four, just a curtained tunnel devoid of the star turn.

Mr Archie turned to the crowd, now getting extremely restless, the clapping turned to shouts seeking an explanation. But there's still nothing just an empty tunnel.

"There my beauties, no zoo for you, off you go back where you all belong," Mr Gerry held open the back gates of the compound; his dear friends hesitated as they crossed the threshold into the darkness of the bush.

"Travel well my friends I shall never forget you," with that Mr Gerry and the security guards pulled the gates closed, watching as the Rendell Four disappeared into the gloom. Free again, with time to make their way deep into the bush before their escape was noticed.

"He's let them go," yelled one of the Rendell security guards into a cell phone, "they've gone back into the bush. What you want me to do boss, not my fault Mr Gerry made me open the gates."

The other security guard, the look on his face showing the strain of Mr Rendell's actions. For Mustafa was not a kind man. Releasing the animals into the night would be treated as treason, even though both were following orders.

Inside the Big Top there was mayhem. Normal sensible people joined the mob culture, many of the audience screaming unintelligibly. Some chanted repeatedly "Rendell Four!" others screamed for their money back. Mr Gerry appeared from the tunnel, and nervously approached his father who handed him the microphone. Gradually the spectators calmed enough for Mr Gerry to speak.

"Ladies and gentlemen, please, please hear me out," he attempted, slowly the yelling subsided. Some individuals continued shouting abuse, only to be challenged by a majority, wishing to hear the explanation Mr Gerry would offer for the absence of the number one attraction.

"Ladies and gentlemen as you can see our final act has not arrived. I have just come from their shelter and found the doors open." Mr Gerry faltered his emotions made it difficult to continue.

There was more shouting, but sections of the audience, who were more reasonable, began calling for calm. Mr Gerry struggled to speak and the audience sensing his emotional state, became silent.

"I cannot lie to you; I released them all back into the wild just before the show started. By now they are way gone into the bush, back to freedom. Isn't that what all you animal rights people wanted?"

There was a mumbling throughout the crowd, TV lights moved closer to Mr Gerry.

"Rendells has always loved and cherished every one of the animals we have trained for our Big Top; there has never been a badly treated animal. So please believe they have lived a better life than most of us. But I cannot see them chained up in a zoo, caged for the rest of their lives, so I made the decision to return them back to nature. You want your money back I guess, we can do that. Rendells has always been the best family circus and we will always be the best circus in Africa."

The silence was deafening. Not a word was uttered, until a lone spectator started a clapping solo. Like a spreading virus, the clapping increased to eventually include most in the Big Top. Mr Gerry's heart-felt speech had won over the spectators, shortly the world would hear about Jango and the circus owner who placed freedom of his animals before profit. Jango was already a household name: a household name with a bike now wandering through the African bush.

# Chapter 17

Three rows back from the ring side, Colonel Ahmed the leader of Princess Leila's mercenaries, silently watched the unfolding events regarding the missing Rendell Four. His plan had been very simple; as soon as the act finished together with his men they would have positioned their Mercedes truck with its cage and crane a short distance from the camp fence. When everyone was settled the two guards on the rear gate close to the shelter would have been drugged, bound and gagged then locked in the hay barn close to the shelter.

The two young elephants would have been given a sedative, not a full blown tranquiliser, making them compliant to walk towards the truck. As he watched

Mr Gerry speak to the packed audience, he understood all their plans had gone badly wrong. Moreover, the news of the world famous bike riding elephant would be on every 24 hour news channel in minutes. Princess Leila and worse still, her husband would want immediate answers. Excuses would be not be tolerated, his group had been paid handsomely to bring back the bike riding elephant, and that's exactly what they were expected to deliver for Prince Halim's new play pen.

Ahmed flicked open his cell phone, punching one of the three stored numbers. Thunderous applause and cheers drowned out the incoming voice so there was no chance of hearing his second in command. Everyone wanted to congratulate Mr Gerry and his father, now pushing forward towards the entrance which should have seen the arrival of the Rendell Four.

There was no way Ahmed could fight his way through the crowds back towards the main exit. He had to go with the flow along with the hordes, making his way past the Rendells, out through the tented tunnel. Away from the deafening roars, he alerted his second in command to search for Jango. The others being of no real interest. It was now search and find their prize. No prize, no bonus, no pay day.

# Chapter 18

The lights from the training compound began to dim as the four edged away carefully from the safety of their home shelter. There had been no hesitation, just one cursory look back at Mr Gerry, who watched them seek the freedom he believed they all wanted. Dangerous as pushing on into the darkness may be, each considered the chances worth taking.

Tonight was a mixed blessing, a full moon being covered most of the time by slow moving storm clouds. Their plan was not difficult, when the full moon was lighting up the countryside they would keep away from open ground. Ensuring they only moved across the open bush, when storm clouds brought the safety of darkness. Brigit was thinking ahead, for they would need to seek cover when daybreak arrived. There was no telling who would be interested chasing after them. Not all man-people were as kind as Mr Gerry, who had released them with a parting tear in his eye.

Sheik Mohamed was leaving nothing to chance. His plans to date had failed. Firstly, Princess Leila was turned away by Mr Gerry, even before discussing the enticing amount she was prepared to pay. Sheik Mohamed's backup plan, which he expected would be required, was planned as an offensive military exercise.

Colonel Ahmed was a seasoned mercenary, with time served for various masters throughout Africa. Ahmed would work for the highest bidder, bringing with him like-minded ex-soldiers whose only interest was cash.

However, this mission was different, at first his men had laughed at being paid $10,000 each just to catch a baby elephant. Now the laughter had now subsided, for they were aware that even with a ten ton Mercedes truck and a couple of Land Rovers they had no idea where the elephants had gone. They could see their prize and the cash disappearing from them.

Ahmed's orders were very clear. Stay put in the chartered Airbus and assistance will arrive. Around the perimeter of the airfield hundreds of rhesus monkeys squawked, welcoming the sun rising over the range of craggy hills a short distance away. Gradually the mixed noises from the animals and birds were drowned out. Increased droning that could only be from a powerful helicopter flying low level towards them, took over. Each man alert at his post fully armed as they waited what could be incoming hostiles. Three took up positions amongst the trees to enable an attack if necessary from their hidden positions.

Screaming from the animals and birds reached panic status as the sound of the helicopter's rotors drew closer. It hovered at the boundary of the airfield waiting to make its appearance. Resplendent in brilliant white with black zebra stripes offering bush camouflage, the chopper settled on the edge of the runway, one hundred metres from the Airbus.

The swirling dust storm began to clear as the engines silenced. From his secured position Ahmed watched as the port side doors of the Black Hawk slid open revealing two men in dark blue flying suits, one carrying a small black attaché case. Ignoring the armed guard, the two pilots made their way towards the ramp of the Airbus, where Ahmed was waiting with four of his mercenaries. Standing in front of Ahmed, they bowed slightly passing over the attaché case. Not a word was spoken.

Ahmed turned from them, making his way into the Airbus to review the contents, gesturing the two pilots to wait. Inside the vast space of the plane, Ahmed carefully opened the case tipping out the contents onto a steel table. There were two items, a sealed brown envelope and a package stuffed with $100 bills. The envelope contained a personal message from the Sheik. Silently Ahmed read and re-read his new orders.

*"Colonel, if you have now opened the sealed letter, our plans to date will have failed. The Black Hawk has two of the best bush pilots; they will not communicate with you regarding their mission. The helicopter is fitted with the latest search and rescue electronic equipment which will ensure this time, there is no failure. Your Mercedes and Land Rover will follow the helicopter and maintain radio silence. The only contact will be coded messages sent to you by the crew. The code language is shown below. Your priority is the young male elephant his code name for this mission is Mr Smith. Disregard the other two elephants and the chimpanzee. Once you have Mr Smith on board you will return to the airfield, pay off your men, load the Mercedes and Land Rovers on to the Airbus and return with Mr Smith. I trust that is clear."*

# Chapter 19

Whatever the situation Benny could not resist larking around. Once an impish chimp, always a mischievous brat. His latest trick jumping between the morula trees, collecting the elephants' favourite nuts and pitching them like coconut shies. Cautious as ever Brigit was keen to keep her friends out of sight. Benny was having the time of his life, enjoying the freedom swinging between whatever greenery would take his weight. Brigit was aware a mischievous chimpanzee would not give them away. In fact from his elevated position Benny would be their lookout. The threesome could be easily identified, each of them still wearing bright red harnesses, which Mr Gerry had forgotten to remove.

However, they were free and making their way almost due north at their own pace. By the third day their confidence had grown, believing they were free and more importantly, that no one was interested in following them. Brigit had virtually no tusks so there was little chance of her being hunted by the evil man-people.

"Brigit, I've never said thank you, for all you've done for us," Jango decided it was time to show his appreciation. "I've had some tough times, but meeting you has made life fun."

"Stop it! You silly boy, don't embarrass me, when Jessica and then you arrived all thoughts I had of escaping disappeared," Brigit replied.

"And what about me you great lump of hide, I've made you laugh haven't I?" Benny questioned, landing on Jango's back.

"Of course you stupid monkey, you're part of the team," Brigit confirmed.

"What we need is to join up with a small herd, I'm sure I can convince the leader to take us. After all, what danger can we be?" Brigit laughed. "Benny you're going to have to use your man-people fingers to take these harness things off us. Even when we join with another herd, we'll still stand out."

"Consider it done great leader," Benny cheekily replied.

At first light the Black Hawk swooped low over a herd of elephants not five miles from Brigit and her friends, its sound just reaching them, causing a watchful Brigit to run from the open bush, seeking shelter. The closest undergrowth she could spot was at least five hundred meters away. On the Black Hawk's electronic sensors another group of animals lit up the screen, just a small group, but fitting into the profile expected of the fugitives. The Black Hawk team had formed a grid pattern systematically searching square by square, now at the extreme west of their search area. From their low level the helicopter lifted to a thousand feet, offering a view of the potential area where they could spot the targets. They were sure the small herd they'd locked on to was their target.

"Follow me, aim for the bushes we can hide there till that flying man thing goes away," Brigit shouted above the thudding of the four bladed rotor blades.

But Jango was transfixed; he had never seen a flying man machine before. It was amazing to think that man-people could fly like birds. Rooted to the spot he was a target for the Black Hawk's on board cameras which now focused on thick red leather straps around Jango's neck. They'd hit pay dirt. There was no place for the little elephant to run: just send a coded message to the Colonel and their job was over. Three days of systematically combing the bush, a simple task with the electronic wizardry on board their Black Hawk, allowing them to pocket $100,000.

"Jango, run don't let the man thing get you," screamed Brigit, knowing there was nothing she could do to help.

Jango just stood rooted to the red earth, hypnotised by the man-people bird flying just above him, the wind stronger than the fierce storms his parents had sheltered him from. His feet stuck, whatever the magic flying beast was doing it had cast a spell over him.

Jessica close behind Brigit, could feel the storm the flying man machine was sending towards them. Her body rocked by its power. Even though they had put distance between themselves and the man machine. Whatever had got into Jango there was nothing they could do. The magic flying machine was now kneeling close to Jango, its wind machine slowing, the gusts now manageable, the clouds of dust settling.

"Nothing to worry about guys, it's a friendly monster. Look its sitting down and quiet. Must be from Mr Gerry checking if we're OK," Jango shouted to his friends across the silence that now had descended, as the Black Hawk waited for further orders.

On the darkened screen on board the Mercedes, a series of messages appeared. "Mr Smith with us – location sector 234 west 20.5 degrees north."

That was it, enough detail for the onboard GPS to lead the convoy directly to Jango. Ahmed pointed at the message to his co-driver, who commenced punching in the information received from the Black Hawk. Within minutes Ahmed's mercenaries had got into the Mercedes and two Land Rovers, ready to follow the direction shown by their on board computer. From the information provided the calculation showed they had a fifteen hour journey before they could start to think of success.

As with most routes across the great expanses of Africa, creation had ensured that you must circumvent craggy terrain, wide ravines, and vast areas cordoned off as either private land or that used by the military to which there was no access. However, there was no hurry, the Black Hawk had found the prize and would not let it out of their electronic sight. Now found, the technology could spot the fugitive elephants again within a matter of minutes.

His curiosity sated, Jango ambled towards Brigit and Jessica, Benny already long gone from the hurricane winds and thunderous noises. Looking back Jango could see the four long stick things had stopped turning and had dropped over the beast. The silence broke as the sliding doors opened; two man-people jumped down pointing a stick at each of the friends showing a small red spot. Each elephant hot marked, now just a matter of time before the Colonel and his men with their hi-tech electronics caught up with the group.

"Jango hurry, we must keep moving," Brigit screamed, already pushing Jessica forward eager to make ground away from the flying man machines.

"It's sleeping Brigit look, it is not going to hurt us," Jango challenged, turning for yet another good look at the extraordinary man machine.

"For the last time Jango, come on, "screamed Brigit.

"OK, but what's the problem Brigit, remember Mr Gerry let us go, so all man-people aren't bad."

Unknown to them, there was no longer any need for the man flying machine to hover like a bird over them. Jango had been hot tagged and unless he could shake off the harness, he was a simple target. There was no escape; he may be the most famous young elephant in the world, his talents marvelled across the globe, but here in the African outback, there was no one to help. Jango would shortly become just another toy in the playground of a spoilt young Arab Prince.

# Chapter 20

As daylight appeared over the South African bush, Ahmed's men loaded their personal equipment in the open Land Rover to prepare for their mission. Apart from ensuring they kept away from hazards which could permanently damage their vehicles, the next stage was simple: A brief rendezvous with the Black Hawk for a one to one de-briefing, before completing the task and it should not prove difficult.

All through the night Jango and his friends pushed on through the moonlight shadows. Without knowing, Brigit had led them through a long 180 degree turn. They had passed within a few hundred metres of the Black Hawk and its sleeping pilots. With daylight now upon them and tired from days of trekking, the shelter of a large clump of dense bushes provided a welcome safe spot to rest.

As the Mercedes lurched forward over the uneven terrain, an electronic beep sounded from the on board computer. There, bright and live was their target not more than one thousand metres distant. Ahmed brought the Mercedes to an immediate halt peering through the roof light to check what the computer had indicated. There, closer than he could have wished, three elephants moved slowly on a parallel reverse course to them.

Although Ahmed's men had fought in a number of campaigns, few had been requested to take prisoners alive. Indeed, never a baby elephant pushing a bicycle. But what the heck, money was money, and swopping powerful firearms for a tranquilliser gun with telescopic sights was fine, the pay was the same. Ahmed had never been a soldier to stand on the hill watching his troops face the enemy. His policy was very much to lead from the front.

For like his men he'd also never shot a wild beast in anger. The vehicle chosen for the next stage was the long wheel base Land Rover, modified with a removable roof panel. A perfect position to fire their tranquilliser gun at the baby elephant. The shot must be perfect just behind Jango's ear, which would sedate him long enough for Ahmed's team to load him into the cage already fixed securely to the

Mercedes.

"Jango keep up, there's another man machine coming this way," Brigit warned as she wearily pushed the pace along, now attempting to drive her two young friends towards the approaching undergrowth, which should give them a chance to re-group.

His body weakened by the sleep inducing drug, Jango's knees had already buckled. He had already been struck behind the right ear by the dart. As consciousness left him, his final roll took him unceremoniously onto his side, a sitting target for the approaching man-people and their machines. There was nothing Brigit and Jessica could do; Jango was either dead or sleeping from the man poison. Furthermore, the man-people had no interest in them, already turning their backs on Jango's two friends.

# Chapter 21

Benny watched from the safety of an umbrella thorn where he had remained as events unfolded. There was no reason to stay with the three wandering elephants, but he was determined to wait his time. Jango had been his friend since they had joined up way back in Zambia. There had been good times and some that had tested his resolve to stay with the crazy tusker. When Jango needed a friend, he knew the timing and opportunity to help would appear. These man-people were not looking for a chimpanzee, their only interest was Jango.

How important and famous Jango had become would never be appreciated by Benny. Every TV news station around the world was running Jango's story; the baby elephant who had been released into the wild by a loving circus owner. Every twenty-four hour news station ran continual VT of Jango on his bike, until after two days the story became old hat and dropped from repeated news items.

That was just the beginning; already Hollywood, taken with the story emerging from Africa, had already commissioned two screen writers to conceive a script for an animated movie. Talk was rife of who would voice the main character and The Hollywood Reporter began speculating who would own the rights to the story, would the Rendells claim copyright?

From the safety of his umbrella thorn Benny watched as the man-people moved their machine close to Jango. Benny was certain that the cage on the biggest man machine would be his friend's new home. Jango had fallen close to a large baobab tree which although not offering cover, would allow Benny to stay close to his friend. As the Mercedes moved along-side Jango, three wide canvas straps were laid on either side of the baby elephant, ready to slide under him in order to lift him into the cage. Benny made his way to the base of the aged baobab, scrambling up between the branches some ten metres above the activity directly below. His was a ring-side view with all the man machines and man-people under his scrutiny.

Their intention was not in doubt, they were going to

lift Jango into the cage which stood taller than them. Puzzled, Benny watched as the long thick stick attached to the machine moved over the sleeping Jango. Eventually the drugged body of Jango rose from the red earth, the man-people carefully guided Jango up and up until he was above the cage. Jango must be important for several man-people arrived with baskets of fruit, fresh grass and water.

One of the man-people holding a large bag climbed inside the cage with Jango. He took several things Benny had never seen before from the bag. After gently touching Jango then lifting his eye lids, the man-person plunged a large needle into Jango's neck. Collecting his strange tools the man-person affectionately rubbed Jango's ear then climbed out of the cage. All around activity increased as the man-people prepared to move. It was decision time for Benny, did he stay put and wish his old friend good luck, or join him for the next stage of their adventure?

"What the heck, I can always play the softy chimp again with the man-people, and we'll both be well fed," Benny whispered.

With that, he swung down from the baobab onto the open top cage, resting on the edge before lowering himself beside Jango.

"Colonel, look!" one of the mercenaries shouted, who had spotted Benny now sitting on Jango's neck, tugging at his ears to wake him.

"That must be the chimp that rode the bike with him," Ahmed laughed, "maybe we get a bonus. I guess he's smarter than we think, must have been following us all the time. Look after him boys, he's our bonus."

"Of course I'm smarter, you dumb man-people, I shall get my friend out of this, just watch," Benny mumbled.

"You will, will you, my monkey friend," Jango had woken from the effect of the antidote which had been pumped into him. "We will get away from these man-people Benny! Thanks you're a real pal. Did they get Brigit and Jessica?"

"They're fine, far away now, these man-people only wanted you," Benny continued.

The Mercedes eased away with its precious cargo, next stop: The airfield.

# Chapter 22

Somalia was a country where poverty was common place with little possibility of employment or regular food supplies for a vast majority of the population. Over the years the income for Somalia's fishermen practically disappeared as international trawlers plundered the fish from their seas. Furthermore, toxic waste was dumped in precious fish breeding waters. Rather than starve with little money to buy food, piracy took over as the major source of income. The Somali term for pirate being "burcad badeed", which means "ocean robber". However, the pirates themselves preferred to be known as "badaadinta badah" or "saviour's of the sea", frequently translated as "coastguard".

Whatever they were called, Somalia became and still remains a euphemism for piracy of the high seas. Commercial shipping travelling through the Indian Ocean and Gulf of Aden, became prized targets for the well-armed and fearless pirates.

Januna Muse and Suguli Jama, both qualified commercial pilots and trained terrorists, joined the pirates from a little know al-Qaeda cell based in Dubai, seeing the prospects of large easy pay days. Both had experience flying converted ex-military transporters mainly from South Africa, through The Middle East and across Northern Europe.

Mustafa had chosen well the team he needed to capture the world famous elephant. For Januna and Suguli were perfect, as his underground information indicated that a rich Sheik from Oman was planning a military style mission involving mercenaries and aircraft.

The Somalian network had informed them of the Airbus A400M charter which had been booked through a small transport office at Pietersburg airport, in northern South Africa. Their attention was drawn to the large amounts of cash that had been paid and the fictitious flight plans filed. In no time their network in Dubai had tracked the charterer to Sheik Mohamed's offices out of Oman. Whatever the Sheik was planning there would be cash involved, he was a man who covered his tracks with bundles of dollar bills.

The chartered Airbus waited the return of their cargo. Both pilots had waited patiently for four days for the Colonel and his men to return. Radio silence frustrated their ability to obtain any real idea of when or indeed where they would be completing their task. Their orders were perfectly clear, when the Colonel's team arrived with the prize, the Airbus should be ready for take-off. Their flight plan would be delivered, only when Colonel Ahmed confirmed he had completed his part of the mission.

Nothing was left to chance, whoever was driving the mission had overall control and it was imperative all parties involved had no idea of the others' orders. A Special Forces covert mission could not have been more carefully planned. For several days the two Airbus pilots had relaxed, never moving more than a few yards from their aircraft. Sleep had taken up much of their time in the hot African sun.

The pilots had no idea for that the last six hours they had been under surveillance from the dense undergrowth, not more than 100 metres from the Airbus. Two sets of eyes had watched every move, patiently waiting their opportunity to take control of the Airbus before the Colonel and his men returned.

Januna and Suguli knew that taking control of the Airbus would not be an issue for two highly trained terrorists. But their action must be swift, removing the slightest chance that either pilot could raise the alarm. There was no necessity to kill them, for tranquillizers would make them sleep for several hours, leaving enough time to be out of South African airspace.

Both Airbus pilots turned over to catch more of the late morning sun, awaiting the return of the Colonel. The attack by the terrorists was silent, swift and effective. Held firmly as they lay face down, hypodermics thrust into their writhing bodies. Within seconds both were sleeping like babies. They would sleep for at least three hours in the undergrowth, the only side-effects being a steaming headache and bites from insects that would find pleasure in feeding on the sleeping bodies.

"Wow look at that man machine," Benny shouted as they rounded the undergrowth on to the runway. "What is it?"

"Whatever it is Benny, that's where we're going," Jango replied standing now against the cage. "Look it's open at the back; I think it's another flying machine."

The open backed Land Rover lined up behind the Mercedes carrying Jango and Benny at the foot of the ramp, waiting for instructions to move. The other hard top Land Rover parked alongside the Airbus, ready for the team to make their way back to Cape Town and to celebrate their success in many of its bars on the beach front.

Ahmed jumped down from the passenger seat of the Mercedes, ordering the truck to make its way into the Airbus. As soon as the Mercedes was on board the Land Rover followed close behind. Inside the Airbus, Ahmed's men moved as a well drilled team locking down the two vehicles, ensuring everything was ready for immediate take-off.

Ahmed inspected both vehicles, checking everything was ready. As he reached Jango and Benny, he ran his hand down Jango's truck, uncertain what to say. For a few moments he stared into the young elephant's face searching for some recognition, but there was nothing. Jango blanked him out, wishing he had muddy water to splash over the man-people who had locked him in this cage, inside the belly of the flying beast.

Several of Ahmed's crew made their way to the cage, two of them bought more fruit and another refilled the water container. Ahmed knew that his task was complete and from here it was over to the pilots. Only the pilots had the information of the destination of the young elephant and his chimpanzee friend.

"All battened down Captain, the elephant's been fed. Oh, and there's a chimp; seems to be the elephant's travelling companion," Colonel Ahmed chuckled.

"Merci Colonel," the only comment returned from the flight deck.

Ahmed knew that he sooner he could get his men away, the sooner they would share out the spoils and then have fun in Cape Town. As the Land Rover passed the end of the runway, Ahmed stopped to look back at the Airbus. It was already positioned, its engines on full throttle, brakes bursting ready for take-off to its next destination.

Suguli, the senior pilot decided he would proceed with his verbal flight plan stating they needed to land at Pietersburg. This would pacify air traffic control and more importantly would stave off any interest from the South African Air Force.

Their precious cargo stowed safely aboard, Januna wandered through the vast storage area of the captured Airbus and stopped to look at the unlikely cargo. So this was the world famous baby elephant that would extract millions from the crazy Sheik! No screaming relatives, no midnight raid by the SAS, just a young herbivore that would pocket them a fortune.

With no traffic control issues, Suguli radioed just to inform that the charter flight already on record was returning to Pietersburg airport, home of the Airbus. Once in the massive hangers they would offload the Mercedes and its cargo. Then wait for darkness to transfer their prize into the awaiting Antonov An-22.

From Pietersburg it would be a short hop to Somalia where the kidnapped prize would be held waiting for the Sheik to deliver their ransom. No one would believe their mission, no fire fights, no moral indignation, the worst they would suffer an outcry from animal charities.

There was no need on this leg for any clandestine course; this was a return to base for a chartered aircraft. The only change being the flight crew. The original crew now recovering from insect bites, having slept for several hours in dense undergrowth surrounding the airfield.

As the giant Airbus took off Jango felt a strange feeling in his stomach. Both uncertain of the new experience Benny clung to his friend as the cage tilted as the aircraft climbed skywards.

"I think we're flying Benny, can't you look out of the window and see where we are?" Jango asked.

Free to climb from the open topped cage, Benny nervously made his way across the back of the Mercedes, then onto the Land Rover, where he could reach a small window.

"Wow, we're way above the trees Jango, you were right we're flying. What do think of that, Jango and Benny the flying twins? Beats our tricks in the circus my man," Benny screamed out from atop the Land Rover. "Now this is one big adventure, don't you think?"

"Just need to get out of this cage, then we can talk

159

about adventure. Still there's food and water, so the man-people can't be too bad," Jango tried to convince himself.

"Jango, as soon as we can get out of here, we will, but together, only together," Benny went on.

# Chapter 23

The Airbus shuddered to a halt inside the ex-military hanger that once housed aircraft from the South African Air Force. Now it was used as a base for a fleet of commercial aircraft, including several ex-Russian Antonov military transporters; stolen by disenchanted Russian soldiers who had taken possession to cover unpaid wages during their time fighting in Afghanistan. The owners of two of the Antonov AN-22 transporters were open to anything to earn a dollar. Gun running, under the cover of aid programs, human traffic another profitable trade, but the latest highly paid transport assisting Somalian pirates shift anything of value to safer locations.

Januma and Suguli considered the Antonov aircraft to be perfect for their activities as many of their flights out of Africa were genuine commercial flights, hauling fruit to the European markets. Knowing the owners of the aircraft did not ask for a detailed flight plan and accepted cash payments, anything that produced cash was fine. This time moving the world famous elephant would be carried out without any questions asked.

Having followed the world wide interest in the baby elephant who rode a small bike; they knew they had captured the hottest ticket in town. Surely the Sheik must have more money than sense to arrange a team of mercenaries, charter an Airbus and build a vast new open-air zoo in Oman, just for a baby elephant. It all proved their cargo would achieve a high ransom value. By now the two original pilots would have been found. Colonel Ahmed would have new orders and his team of mercenaries, would be on even more serious money to re-capture the world famous elephant.

Each day their ransom price would increase. However, the timing of the announcement of their captured prize must be carefully calculated. First they must move the Mercedes and its cargo onto the aging Antonov, already fuelled, ready to fly north at low level away from the eyes of South African radar. Once out of South African airspace they would continue to fly low level over the Limpopo into

Zimbabwean airspace then turn due east across Mozambique till they settled over the Indian Ocean. From there they would fly due north, keeping the coast of Africa on their left side until arriving near Chisimayu in Somalia, where they would land on a quiet ex-military air strip. Once safe in Somalia they would require the protection of the pirate leaders, agreeing a share of the ransom for the world famous elephant.

# Chapter 24

Klaus Binderfeld had always been proud of his German ancestry having developed a typically German wish to have everything in his life efficient. From the moment he'd spotted Jango's amazing bike riding skills he could smell the money to be made. Maybe a deal with his royal friend, Prince Harold, whose home in Nigeria was stuffed with everything his vast wealth could buy. Like many Nigerians, Prince Harold claimed royalty dating back many generations. But in truth the real royal birth lines had failed to have any real power before he was born. But whatever the truth of his birthright, he had made vast fortunes from trading coal, coke and oil.

"I've tracked the young elephant your highness.

Amateurs leave clear tracks," Klaus advised Prince Harold by phone. "My network of spies - well that's what they like to called - have tracked the elephant to a flight by Colonel Ahmed's team into Pietersburg. Quite what they intend to do then we're not sure. I think we shall take control of the beast there. Then we can talk money."

Klaus was equally as efficient using the information he had collected. Once he knew the Airbus carrying Jango would land at Pietersburg airport a team of ex-military men from the Congo, prepared for any task, would be put in place. Klaus's team would overpower the pilots, ensuring they were not badly hurt, then move Jango to a farm just east of Pretoria, from where he could then begin discussing the price of freedom for the famous young elephant. Klaus could already see at least two possible buyers. But others would come forward to acquire the most famous elephant in the world.

# Chapter 25

"What do you think they're doing Benny?" Jango asked his friend, the Mercedes now off loaded from the Airbus into the massive hanger, awaiting its next destination.

"Wait here Jango," Benny whispered to his friend, "Let me listen to them, look over there more man-people."

"Wait here, you great fool, what else can I do," Jango laughed from inside the cage, "go on but please be careful, I don't think they're friendly man-people."

No more than twenty metres away Suguli and Januna were deep in conversation with six large black man- people. To begin with Benny could hear nothing but a mumble from both sides of the conversation. The body language indicated this was not a friendly tête-à-tête. Silently Benny scampered way across the top of the Land Rover until he was within a few metres, looking down on the six man-people.

"We need more money for moving the elephant into the Antonov," one of the large black man people shouted at Januna, their faces close together.

"He's on all the news programs, there's a big reward for him," another black man-person shouted.

Januna and Suguli said nothing, their highly trained close contact skills at the ready to take control of the situation. Benny could sense they could soon have new captors; the odds firmly stacked against the two kind man-people they had travelled with in the flying machine. Behind the Somalians, two more black man-people carrying long sticks, crept silently closer, clearly intent on attacking the pilots.

Benny had to make a decision, hoping Jango would agree. Benny's screech and bouncing on the Land Rover roof had the necessary effect. Together the six black man-people turned towards Benny who was performing a mad roof top dance. Alive to the situation Januna and Suguli pounced on two of the black man-people. But their efforts were in vain as the other two man-people had crept up behind them and crashed their sticks onto them, rendering them unconscious. Benny's plan had backfired. The black man-people now firmly in control, dragged the limp bodies of the pilots to an inspection pit where they were unceremoniously dumped.

From the shadows of the hanger a tall man smartly dressed in a black suit walked slowly towards the eight black men.

"Excellent work my friends and you followed my script perfectly. When their bosses question them, they'll tell of greedy workers blackmailing for extra money to load the cargo, perfect!" Klaus advised his men. "Let's get the cage covered and take the little chap down to the farm, now hurry."

"What happened Benny?" Jango shouted as Benny reached the cage. "So much shouting, tell me!"

"Our friends from the man flying machine were attacked then dumped into a hole in the ground," Benny screamed, shaking from the violence he'd witnessed. "I think these other bad man-people are taking us away."

"Benny, run now, I'll be fine, it's obviously me they want, not you," Jango pleaded.

"Run, what you talking about, Oh no, this is getting interesting Jango. Together my tusker friend, together."

Back inside the cage Benny sat on Jango's neck like a hunt jockey. The two of them watched as the man-people moved towards them with a large black sheet which was dragged across the cage and tied firmly at each corner. To the passing observer, there would be no indication what the Mercedes was carrying, apart from a large box covered by a black plastic sheet. The two animals were prisoners within a darkened cage, only a tiny shaft of light available through one badly tied corner.

So far Jango and Benny had been treated well, even when held in captivity. But there was a malevolent feel about their new captors. Unaware if they were flying, driving or on the water, the black plastic sheet had created a disorientating effect. Neither having the slightest idea, where they were travelling nor what was happening outside their prison cage. All they could do was wait. All they could do was guess and trust their captures were kind man-people.

Every few minutes they heard a roar as they passed another man machine, sometimes a horn sounded. From his near-miss crossing the man road during his travels with Whisper, Jango remembered these sounds. In the flying machine, although noisy, they had been able to rest as the journey was smooth with no bumping around. But this was very different, the cage shook and bounced with no respite. All they could do was lean against the bars for support in an attempt to stop themselves from crashing around.

Jango thumped heavily against the front of the cage. Deafening screeches from crushing metal coupled with an explosion of flying broken Mercedes parts, together with man-people screams filled the air. Both the mangled Mercedes and a VW Kombi were completely split in two from a head on collision. Jango fell from the top of the cage, his trunk sliced open as he rolled over and over away from the wreckage.

The first glimpse of morning sun was just appearing over the bush, offering sufficient light to show the horror of the impact between the two vehicles. A number of injured man-people were strewn across the wide arterial road, several staggering around, dazed by the horror of the crash. Although badly cut, Jango was alive. However, Benny was missing, he was nowhere to be seen amongst the wreckage.

"Benny!... Benny!... Where are you?" Jango struggled back towards the heap of broken metal. Destruction everywhere! Crumpled man-people, some with broken legs, some holding twisted arms, injured bodies littered all over the highway.

Jango eased closer to the cage that had brought them across Africa together. Benny could have left him, but had stayed his closest companion. The black sheet which had covered the cage was now in shreds, the cage tipped on its side.

"Jango, I'm here," Benny's weakened voice was just audible above the screams and sobbing around the site of the accident.

"I've got you my ugly monkey friend," Jango screamed moving close to the twisted cage where Benny was lying.

"Benny, hold on I'll have to move the cage and you'll have to creep out, OK?" Jango cried.

Jango's scream was terrifying as he wrapped his trunk around the cage bars, forgetting he was carrying a long open wound along at least half his trunk.

"Stop you stupid tusker, the man-people will be here soon to get me out," Benny struggled with the words. "Can you hear that noise Jango, it's the man machines coming to help.

"Benny, you're nearly free, help me move the food boxes off your legs! Come on! This is our escape my monkey friend."

In the distance police sirens screamed out as they approached the horror spread across the main road from Pietersburg to Pretoria. Help was nearby.

Fuel had spilt across the highway spreading around the Kombi batteries. The fire was instant engulfing the remains of the Kombi, accompanied by screams as two man-people tried to douse the flames lapping around their trapped legs. Jango had always been petrified of fire and could now smell the inferno. Again he tried to wrap his trunk around the food containers. This time he resisted the need to scream as the pain again shot through his body.

It would only be a matter of time before the flames licking around the wreckage reached the Kombi's ruptured fuel tank. When it came the explosion threw flames high in the air, enveloping both vehicles. The blast knocked Jango sideways, away from the cage and into the bush. Painfully he pulled himself to his feet and stared at the horrific scene. Through the raging flames he could just make out the cage. Benny, was nowhere to be seen. As its fuel tank ignited a further explosion shattered the remaining section of the Mercedes. Surely no person or animal could survive the ferocious flames that now engulfed the area? Suddenly somewhere Benny's screams could be heard. Jango could not let his best friend not end his days on a South African highway.

Surrounded by the inferno roaring away in front of him, Jango felt powerless. All he could do was watch, hoping his friend had not burnt to death in the flames. His bleeding trunk needed urgent attention, the wound was excruciating and he shook with pain. He knew he had to find a watering hole with heaps of mud and treat himself. Exactly as he had done for Tulu. Jango was now alone for the first time in his life.

His parents were somewhere on the Serengeti. Whisper had returned to the wild to confirm his status as king of the jungle. His brother Hector would be wallowing in whatever mud he could find. And what about Tulu? He would have caught up with his herd, probably deciding which lady to chase. Brigit had found a family with Jessica. There was no need for them ever to perform in a circus ring again, the wide expanses of Africa were open to them.

As Jango played out his short life, a further explosion lifted the broken parts into the air. Jango watched as everything appeared to happen in slow motion as heaps of metal shot skywards, and crashed to earth in a deafening clatter.

Jango turned back towards the cage, now settled well away from the main source of the flames, by the force of the blast. Still, there was no sight of his friend, his faithful companion throughout the shared ups and downs as they crossed Africa. Benny had many opportunities to make off into the bush; on a number of occasions Jango had urged him to leave. However, the he had stayed, some days irritating everyone as he chattered endlessly like a broken record, but always loyal.

Jango had no idea that he was the most famous elephant, probably the best known animal, in the world. Despite all his fame he was lost and all alone in the wide open spaces of the South African bush. With a massive price on his head, how long would it be before someone would find him? Certainly the Sheik would never give up. Colonel Ahmed would be given fresh orders, bribed with even more dollars to capture Jango for the private zoo.

Both Jango and Benny were ignorant of the fate of the two Somalian pilots who had been attacked in the hanger. If they were dead, surely others would follow and take their place. If people were prepared to kill each other to watch him ride his two-wheeler, then all the man-people had gone mad, he would never be safe.

His father told him many times that man-people were the only danger for elephants, but that was for a grown elephant, or so he thought. After all he had experienced Jango was now fully aware the real danger facing a young African elephant could only be the greed of the evil man- people.

Jango could just make out the fearful wailing of a number of fast approaching man trucks. He was determined to search one last time for his chimpanzee friend before they reached him. He winced from the searing pain pulsing from the wound extending down his trunk as he turned to make his way back towards the upturned cage.

Through the slowly clearing clouds of smoke, he could make out the wreckage of his two- wheeler.

He struggled against his pain to reach his two-wheeler. It was covered in blistering bubbles of burning paint, the saddle gone, both tyres smouldering. Jango made his way off the road into the bush where he ripped up roots of as much grass as he could manage. Armed with the grass wrapped round his trunk, he pulled the remains of his two-wheeler back off the road into the bush. There, amongst the long grass, struggling to hide from the man-people, Jango collapsed, overwhelmed by the pain from his severely lacerated trunk.

"You gonna lie there all day, or we gonna escape? Now I gotta plan young tusker," a blackened Benny shook his friend.

"That you? You crazy monkey, where've you been hiding from me?" Jango struggled with the words, his vision hazy from the pain.

"We have to move. We cannot let the man- people take us again! Leave it me let's get going before the sun gets too high. Oh and sorry but that two-wheeler has seen better days. It stays right here Jango! New adventures my boy, now let's find some water and mud and get you mended."

The End.

The illegal killing of elephants and the trade in their ivory is out of control across Africa, undermining ecosystem integrity, economic development and the rule of law. In the last three years 100,000 elephants have been brutally killed to supply ivory to illegal markets in Asia. Poaching, combined with a shrinking habitat from natural resource extraction, have pushed this majestic animal to the brink of extinction. Unless urgent action is taken, the African elephant will die out in the wild within our lifetime.

**Space for Giants** is an international conservation charity with 15 years of experience in the conservation and management of African elephants and the landscapes they depend on. We aim to secure a future for the largest mammals on earth forever, to be enjoyed by humanity forever, by ensuring that they have the space and security to live and move freely in the wild forever. We work on the ground every day to provide a secure future for elephants, the places they live and the species that share their range.

Spaceforgiants.org  info@spaceforgiants.org

Space for Giants is an international conservation charity, registered in the UK (charity no: 1139771) and USA (EIN: 47-1805681) and Kenya governed by a volunteer Board of Trustees.

15% of the author's profit from the sale of this book shall go to The Space for Giants Charity.

SPACE FOR
GIANTS
www.spaceforgiants.org